He was sham

If he was brazen e... her, then Jade was going to be just as bold and watch.

Kyle met her challenge, and with all the lazy, practiced ease of a male stripper he gyrated his hips and shimmied the jeans down his thighs. The only thing missing from his act was a G-string. Instead, he wore striped boxer shorts. That single article of clothing saved Jade's quickly evaporating sanity.

His chest was wide and powerful. A light sprinkling of golden hair swirled around flat brown nipples and arrowed down a lean torso and belly. His waist was trim, his body hard and honed. He was masculine perfection. He was everything she'd ever dreamed of in a man, a breath-stealing combination of sin and sensuality.

"More?" he asked. Kyle's fingers snapped the elastic band of his shorts, drawing her attention to the only part of him he hadn't bared, but seemed more than willing to.

He was so bad, and he knew it, too.

Dear Reader,

I have to confess—I love going to yard sales and I seldom come home empty-handed. Once, while I was rummaging through a box of books, I began to wonder what would happen if a personal diary accidentally ended up in the wrong place and someone purchased it....

From this germ of an idea, *Private Fantasies* was created. When Kyle Stevens comes across his gorgeous neighbor's journal of private fantasies, he can't resist. You see, he's incredibly attracted to Jade, but other than an occasional flirtatious encounter in the lobby of their complex, she won't have anything to do with him. Ah, but now he's got an intimate insight into who Jade really is...and all her needs, dreams and desires.

What Kyle does with those fantasies will shock and thrill you. Imagine having your own fantasy man, one who knows exactly what you want and need, physically and emotionally. Sounds deliciously forbidden, doesn't it? But what happens when those fantasies begin to merge with reality? And what will happen when that personal, intimate journal threatens to destroy the best thing that ever happened to Kyle?

To find out, turn the page and lose yourself in the fantasy....

Best wishes,

Janelle Denison

P.S. I've really enjoyed writing about the amorous escapades of the Stephens sisters, Mariah and Jade, in *Private Pleasures* and *Private Fantasies*. I'd love to hear if you enjoyed them as much as I did. You can write to me c/o Harlequin Books, 225 Duncan Mill Road, Don Mills, Ontario, Canada M3B 3K9.

PRIVATE FANTASIES
Janelle Denison

Harlequin Books

TORONTO • NEW YORK • LONDON
AMSTERDAM • PARIS • SYDNEY • HAMBURG
STOCKHOLM • ATHENS • TOKYO • MILAN
MADRID • WARSAW • BUDAPEST • AUCKLAND

To Jeanie and Gary Denison, for being such great in-laws, and for raising such a caring son, and teaching him the value of family. I'm reaping the benefits.

A big thanks to my editor, Brenda Chin; this book wouldn't have been possible without your enthusiasm, encouragement and support.

And, as always, to Don, who makes me laugh and smile and enjoy life. Happy eleventh anniversary!

ISBN 0-373-25782-1

PRIVATE FANTASIES

Copyright © 1998 by Janelle Denison.

This edition published by arrangement with Harlequin Books S.A.

® and TM are trademarks of the publisher. Trademarks indicated with ® are registered in the United States Patent and Trademark Office, the Canadian Trade Marks Office and in other countries.

Printed in U.S.A.

1

HE WAS READING her mail again.

Jade Stevens advanced into the lobby of her condominium complex, eyeing the man lounging on the sofa in the sitting area near the residents' mailboxes as he flipped through *her* Victoria's Secret catalog. Kyle Stephens had too much nerve, too much charm and way too much interest in her. The first two she could deal with. It was the third she couldn't seem to discourage, no matter how many times she rebuffed his advances and turned down his outrageous, flirtatious proposals.

Any other man would have backed off long ago. Not Kyle. After twenty-three rejections he was still going strong, dauntless and bold as ever.

He had trouble written all over that gorgeous, lean body of his—from his reckless grin and seductive baby blues, to his unapologetic approach that should have irritated her, but stimulated her instead. Which was enough to alert her to keep her distance emotionally. So far she'd been successful.

During the past six months, they'd developed a friendship of sorts. Not by *her* choice, but out of necessity. Since her name was Jade Stevens, and his was Kyle Stephens, and their addresses were so similar—hers 321 Camilia and his 312 Camilia—their mail was continuously getting mixed up and dropped in each other's box.

She released a sigh of breath and prepared herself for

Kyle's brand of trouble. "Hello, Kyle," she said pleasantly.

"Mmm," he replied distractedly.

Which wasn't surprising, considering how engrossed he was in her lingerie catalog. He turned the page to the next spread, and let out a low, appreciative whistle—the same sexy whistle he'd given her a time or two.

Stopping at the bank of metal mailboxes, she set her attaché case on the plush mauve carpeting and dug through her purse for her mailbox key. "I take it we've got another new mail carrier on our route."

"Yeah." His voice was a rich, silky rumble that did delicious, wicked things to her nerve endings.

He lowered the women's mail-order magazine just enough for her to glimpse eyes filled with mischief and sin, and a bad-boy grin creasing the corners of his mouth. Thick, roguishly long, tawny-colored hair tousled around his head in its normal, windblown fashion. He wore what she'd learned was his bartending attire: black jeans and T-shirt with his bar's name The Black Sheep emblazoned across his wide chest in white lettering, along with black leather boots, propped negligently on the coffee table in front of the sofa.

"This one was kind enough to put this very stimulating piece of mail into my box. And here I thought you were a nice girl," he chastised softly, the gleam in his eyes turning as wicked as the low timbre of his voice. "Though I have to warn you, I find naughty *extremely* exciting."

An involuntary shiver coursed through her, and she turned her back on him to open her metal box. "In your dreams, Kyle."

He chuckled. "Wouldn't be the first time, sweetheart. But I'm certain reality will be ten times better than in my dreams."

The man's confidence astounded her. "Don't waste your time thinking about it. It's not going to happen."

"Oh, I wouldn't be too sure about that," he drawled lazily. "One of these days you're gonna throw that caution of yours to the wind and take me up on my offer to go out on a date. And when you finally give in, you're gonna wonder why you waited so long."

She reached for her mail while casting him a pointed look over her shoulder. "Do you ever take no for an answer?"

He tilted his head. A speculative gleam entered his eyes as he oh-so-slowly swept his gaze down the length of her, a visual caress that left a trail of heat in its wake. Then he countered with, "Do you ever let down that guard of yours long enough to let a man get close?"

Not any more. Ignoring his direct challenge and his even more discerning stare, she glanced back at the mail in her hand. Out of all the men she'd encountered since her breakup with Adam three years ago—and she encountered plenty at Roxy's, a nightclub she frequented—Kyle was by far the most daring and forthright. He challenged her defenses and brazenly confronted the emotional boundaries she'd established between them, barriers that usually dissuaded men's advances.

"Looks like I have a few pieces of your mail," she said, shifting to a safer, more mundane topic.

She heard the sofa creak as he stood, then his hushed steps on the padded carpet as he started toward her. Ignoring the crazy leap of her pulse, she continued sorting through the letters, periodicals and advertisements for his mail.

Concentrating on the simple task proved futile. Unable to see him as he approached from behind, she felt at a distinct disadvantage, but refused to move or turn around and let him know just how much he affected her.

She might not be able to see him, but she could *feel* him closing in on her. Awareness fluttered deep in her belly, and a traitorous anticipation tingled just beneath the surface of her skin. He stopped behind her, bracing a hand on the wall to her left, and she almost lost her grip on their mail.

He didn't touch her, but then he didn't have to. The heat of his body settled along her spine, over her bottom, and traveled the length of her legs where they extended from the short, silky sarong skirt she wore. She was acutely aware of him as a man, the lean, muscular strength of his body, his warm male scent and the hazardous level of desire he evoked within her.

Despite her resolve not to be, she was attracted to Kyle Stephens. And tempted. And that was a dangerous, destructive combination for her, one she refused to be enticed by again.

She held her breath, clutched their mail, and waited, wondering what he intended next, even while she searched her turning-to-mush mind for a way to stop this madness. This was, by far, his boldest move yet, and it *had* to stop!

But there was no stopping Kyle.

He lowered his head to the side of hers and his free hand stretched around her waist to hold the Victoria's Secret catalog in front of her. The magazine was folded back to a page advertising luxurious lotions, fragrant sprays, scented soaps and body washes. Jade recognized her favorite scent, *peach hyacinth*.

"Now I know why you always smell like peaches," he murmured, his breath tickling her ear. He dipped his head lower, grazing his chin along her neck. Inhaling deeply, he groaned low in his throat, like a man savoring the scent of something decadent and forbidden. "Ripe, *juicy* peaches. I can't help but wonder if you taste just as sweet."

Her breath left her in a whoosh. Yanking the incriminating evidence from his hand, she turned and slapped his own mail against his chest.

"Here's your mail," she said evenly. How could he look so calm, composed, *amused even*, when he had her unraveling from the inside out? "I'll be sure to contact the post office Monday morning so they can let the new carrier know about the problem."

He folded the advertisement around the few letters she'd given him and slipped the mail into the back pocket of his jeans. "I don't mind exchanging our mail."

She'd bet he didn't, but she *did* mind. Especially since it was getting more difficult to shake her attraction to him. The man just didn't *shake!*

Turning and presenting him with her back in dismissal, she shut her mailbox and retrieved her key. But before she could move away, two large, strong hands settled on her shoulders and eased toward her neck in a slow, sensuous massage. She automatically stiffened, shocked at his intimate caress.

"You're so tense," he said, his tone a trifle mocking. "Long day at the office?"

Oh, Lord, his hands were pure magic on her skin. Skillfully and firmly rubbing taut muscles, then gentling into a luxurious kneading that had her softening, dissolving beneath the mastery of his incredible touch. She bit back a groan and suppressed the urge to roll her head forward to give him better access to the tight muscles at the nape of her neck.

"It's, uh..." She caught her breath as his thumbs

pressed between her shoulder blades and rolled upward. An automatic, appreciative rumbling purr rose up in her throat. She promptly swallowed it. "It's been a long week."

He continued his wonderful massage. "What do you say you come by The Black Sheep tonight and have a drink, relax, unwind.... I'll have Bruce close up and you and I can take a stroll along the beach and talk...."

His brand of conversation, all sexy innuendo and sweet-talking charm, would inevitably turn into more. And his hands were talking plenty, telling her he'd be a generous, giving lover.

Not that it mattered.

Not that she cared.

She slipped from under his hands before she did something incredibly stupid...like agree to meet him for a drink. "I've got other plans," she said, using the business-like tone she reserved for the pushy clients who came into her and her sister's design firm, Casual Elegance.

He leaned a shoulder against the bank of mailboxes, unaffected by her brush-off. "Roxy's?" he guessed, having caught her a few times on a Friday evening when she'd been on her way out of the lobby to the nightclub.

"I have work to do, not that it's any of your business." And a long, hot bath she wanted to take. She *was* tense, but now for an entirely different reason than her long week. Stuffing her mail into her attaché, she grasped the leather handles and started around Kyle toward the main entrance into the complex.

He followed by her side. "Don't you know you're supposed to leave work at the office? All work and no play is going to make Jade very dull."

"Trust me," she said, giving her head a sassy shake and

making her chin-length hair sway along her jaw. "You add more than enough excitement to my 'dull' existence."

His fingers curled around her elbow, giving her the choice of halting or being yanked back into his arms. She did the smart thing and stopped.

His thumb stroked the soft skin of her inner elbow. "Do I?"

She forgot what they'd been discussing, enthralled by the darkening of his blue eyes, as warm and arousing as his touch. "Do you what?"

He blinked lazily. "Add excitement to your life?"

More than he knew, and more than she'd ever verbally admit. Sighing, she extricated her arm from his gentle grasp. "I only meant that I never know what to expect from you."

He grinned, that wonderfully sexy smile that lit up his eyes and tempted her common sense. "If you went out with me you'd know exactly what to expect. A great time."

She inclined her head. "You are a persistent one, aren't you?"

He shrugged those broad shoulders of his. "Only when I see something I like."

"And if I told you I wasn't interested, tonight or in the future?"

He considered her question for two whole heartbeats. "Then I'd have to say that mouth of yours is lying."

She touched her tongue to her bottom lip before realizing what she'd done. "And if I told you you had a giant ego?" she asked, unwilling to let him have the last word.

"I'd have to tell you you're absolutely right," he replied unrepentantly, and leaned closer. "Why should I give up when I'm so close to wearing down your resistance?"

Her mouth twitched with a smile she refused to let

loose. "The answer is still no." She started again toward the entrance leading to the units, and when he stayed behind, she glanced back and gave him a brisk wave that tinkled the gold bracelets on her arm. "Have a good night, Kyle."

He pressed a hand dramatically to his chest and gave her a pained look. "You're breaking my heart, honey."

Without a doubt, *he'd* break *hers.* "I'm certain I'm not the first, or the last."

Kyle grinned as he watched Jade walk away. Tilting his head, he admired the slow, sexy sway of her hips covered in scarlet red silk, and those incredibly long legs that ended in three-inch heels. His gut tightened as a hundred fantasies sprang to mind, one in particular of Jade wearing one of those silky teddy things he'd seen in her lingerie catalog, and him slowly stripping it away. And along with the scrap of lace, he'd shed that cool reserve she wore like armor and discover every one of her sweet, feminine secrets.

In your dreams, Kyle.

Despite himself, he chuckled. There was more to Jade Stevens than met the eye, and he was fascinated enough to pursue an attraction he'd proved minutes ago was mutual. She was the most exciting, intriguing woman he'd ever met, strong but utterly feminine, and full of a fire and sass that continually surprised him.

It was that damnable emotional barrier of hers he couldn't seem to get around. And he'd tried every conceivable way in the past six months to shatter that restraint of hers.

She turned the corner and was out of sight, but she still lingered in Kyle's mind. She always did.

"One of these days, Jade, I'm gonna figure out what

makes you tick," he murmured to himself in the deserted lobby. "And when I do, you're gonna be all mine."

KYLE STARED IN DISBELIEF at the burgundy bound journal filled with a collection of intimate fantasies, stunned that something so personal and revealing had found its way into his hands—at a yard sale, no less.

Remaining crouched in front of a box full of cookbooks, popular hardbacks and other miscellaneous paperbacks, and keeping his back to the people milling through the other items set out for sale, he casually opened the front flap. The name Jade Stevens was written on the inside cover, along with a date of close to three years ago. He drew a deep breath, and giving in to curiosity, he skimmed through the journal, wanting to read what else lay between the pages—and discover more of Jade's deepest secrets and desires.

Unable to help himself, he thumbed to the beginning and read the first entry:

The waiting was over.

Out of the shadows, he appeared at the edge of the pond where she swam, the silvery cast of moonlight silhouetting his tall, lean build and glinting off his light, tawny-colored hair. He was everything she'd ever dreamed of in a man, a breath-stealing combination of sin and sensuality.

Magnificently naked, he dove into the water, sending rippling waves of water lapping against her bare shoulders, as cool and sensuous as a lover's caress. Her heart pounded in her chest as she waited for him....

He broke the surface an arm's length away, rising out of the water until it pooled around his waist. His dark magnetism entranced her, seduced her, yet she knew she had no reason to fear him.

"What are you doing here?" she whispered.

Midnight eyes glittered with a heat that started a slow ache within her. "You invited me, remember?" She did invite him. Many times. She just never expected him to come. "You're a fantasy, nothing more."

"You created me, Jade." He held out his hand, palm up, an invitation to trust. "Swim with me."

Knowing she had complete control over the fantasy, she placed her fingers in his palm and glided toward him. The contact of slick, naked skin was searing, breathtaking and exciting. Her breasts swelled and tingled against the solid wall of his chest, and a liquid heat settled low in her belly.

His mouth moved near her ear. "Now close your eyes...and feel."

Biting back a moan of pleasure, she succumbed to the stroking of his hands, the feel of his lips against her throat and moving lower. She wanted to go with the impulse and revel in the sheer enjoyment of being undisciplined. Wild. No restraints, no reservations. With him, she knew there were no restrictions....

Feeling the slow thrum of desire coursing through his veins, Kyle closed the book. A slow smile curved his mouth. A journal filled with private fantasies at a yard sale was obviously a mistake on Jade's part, but one he intended to use to his advantage. What he held in his hands was an invaluable insight to the woman who tried so hard to keep a tight rein on the fire and passion he'd known simmered beneath the surface.

Jade hadn't fooled him for a minute, and now he had proof of that banked sensuality. And ammunition.

He'd just discovered what made Jade tick.

Shoving the journal into the box in front of him and burying it beneath the other books, he cast a sideways look at Jade. Their relationship had started out as a light flirtation due to their mail situation, had progressed into a mutual attraction she wouldn't succumb to, and had evolved into an obsession he couldn't shake. Now he hoped their relationship would become much more.

Finished dealing with her yard-sale customer, Jade stood talking to another woman who held a toddler in her arms. Warm rays of sunshine filtered through the leaves and branches on the tree overhead, weaving golden highlights through the rich brown strands of her hair. Wispy bangs framed her face and softened her features.

She wore a bright fuchsia halter top that left her midriff bare, and turquoise shorts that displayed slim thighs and tanned, shapely legs. The bright, colorful straps on her leather sandals matched her expressive outfit, along with coordinating loop earrings and bangle bracelets.

The blonde next to her motioned in his direction and Jade looked his way, surprise lighting her vivid green eyes. Jade said something to the other woman, then lifted a brow at him that clearly asked what he was doing there.

His original intent had been to return another piece of mail, but she'd been busy with a customer wanting to negotiate the price on a headboard with a built-in bookcase. So he'd stopped at a box full of books to look through until she was done with her current transaction...and had found something more stimulating than self-help books, romance novels and cookbooks.

Hefting the entire box of books into his arms, he approached the trio. As he neared, he noticed a slight resemblance in features between Jade and the blonde. He noted the other woman's eye color, a striking blue, and wondered if that was Jade's true eye color as well. Jade's eye color seemed to change every time he saw her, dramatic, bold hues too intense to be natural. He'd yet to decide which shade was the real Jade.

Another interesting facet he was determined to expose.

"Tell me you're not moving," he said, waving a hand toward the furnishings for sale. "Or you'll break my heart for sure."

"It's in with the new and out with the old," she said, eyeing the box he carried. "I just redecorated my place."

"I'm relieved to hear that." More relieved than she'd ever know, because he didn't relish the thought of having to try and find her new address. That he'd go to such an extreme for a woman told him he was in way over his head, but he was already a goner where Jade was concerned.

He stopped a few feet away. "How much do you want for the books?"

Jade glanced into the open carton at the cookbooks and romance novels piled at the top. She frowned up at him, clearly baffled by his choice of reading material. "You want the *whole* box?"

He couldn't very well flash the journal in front of her and expect her to sell it to him. "My great aunt likes to read romances and I like to cook," he explained, leaving out the little fact that his great aunt lived in Detroit, not nearby in California, and was blind as a bat.

Jade stepped forward and rummaged through the books. Kyle resisted the urge to jerk the box out of her reach, hoping all the while that she wouldn't discover the leather-bound journal buried somewhere in-between. She barely skimmed the pile of hardbacks on top before she turned to the blonde and asked, "Aren't some of these books yours, Mariah?"

"Most of them are the ones you told me to clear out of that bookcase headboard you just sold." Mariah set the little girl in her arms on the blanket spread out in front of her. The baby crawled to a toy and began playing with it, gurgling and drooling contentedly. "And I threw in some of my old cookbooks I'd left behind after marrying Grey."

Jade gave an exaggerated shudder. "I'll *pay* you to take the cookbooks off my hands."

He chuckled. "Not much of a cook, huh?"

"Not unless you like indigestion for dessert," the blonde piped in, wrinkling her nose.

Jade glared at the other woman, but there was clearly a close bond between them.

He shifted the box under his arm, keeping his gaze on the other woman. "I take it you've had firsthand experience with Jade's cooking."

"Um, you could say that. I guarantee, it's not worth risking your life over." The blonde held out her hand, put on a welcoming smile, and introduced herself. "I'm Mariah, Jade's sister."

Kyle set the box down by his side and clasped Mariah's hand. "I'm Kyle Stephens with a 'ph,'" he clarified with a grin. "I'm a neighbor of Jade's. It's a pleasure to meet you." He glanced down at the baby who was staring up at him with her mother's big blue eyes. "And this little princess must be yours, too."

Mariah beamed with pride. "She's my daughter, Kayla."

Crouching to Kayla's level, he gave in to the impulse to caress his hand over the blond curls framing her cherubic face. Downy soft hair sifted through his fingers, and he breathed in the scent of baby powder. Man, he'd forgotten how sweet babies smelled, and how their precious smiles could make him soften inside like a big marshmallow. It had been years...seventeen to be exact.

The subtle longing he experienced surprised him, grabbing at an instinct deep and buried, but certainly not forgotten. It made him wish, for a brief moment, that he'd made different choices in his past.

"Hello, doll," he murmured in a gentle tone, not wanting to frighten her.

Kayla let out a squeal of delight and blew him a raspberry. He laughed at her antics and glanced back up at Mariah. "She's beautiful, just like her mom."

Mariah blushed at his compliment. "Thank you."

"Personally I think she takes after her aunt." Jade bent down and gave her niece a quick tickle in the ribs. "Don'tcha, sweetie?"

Kayla giggled, and grabbed at the bright, colorful bracelets jangling on her aunt's wrist. "J-J!" she gurgled, a happy grin splitting her face.

"See, I told you," Jade teased her sister, her smile smug.

"The only thing she inherited from her aunt is her ornery temperament," Mariah gibed.

Kyle grinned at the easy friendship between siblings, a closeness he had never shared with his own brother and stepsister. Straightening, he let his gaze climb up the length of Jade's sleek legs, the curve of her hips, the fullness of her breasts, until his eyes met and held hers. "I can't imagine you having an ornery bone in your entire body."

Her brows rose and her cheeks colored, but before she could formulate a response, Mariah cut in with, "Try living with her. Trust me, she's got herself a temper."

Jade just rolled her eyes. "How about ten dollars for the

box of books?" she offered, steering the conversation back to business.

To him the journal was priceless, not that he was about to tell her she was undercutting herself. "It's a deal." Withdrawing his wallet from the back pocket of his jeans before she changed her mind, he riffled through his billfold for the appropriate amount of cash and handed her the money.

"Enjoy the books," she said, taking the bills from him.

"Oh, I plan to." *Every last sultry, intimate fantasy*, he thought.

"I almost forgot," he said as he tucked his wallet away and withdrew an envelope from his other back pocket. "Looks like I got your electric bill by mistake today."

"That one you could have kept," she teased.

He turned the bill over in his hands, not ready to hand it over yet. "You know, there's only one way to permanently remedy this problem we seem to be having with our mail."

Jade glanced at her sister to see if she was still watching the exchange, which she was with interest, then glanced back at him. The caution in her eyes told him she knew he was about to flirt. "Which would be...?"

He smiled, a slow reckless grin. "Move in together."

Her mouth twitched to suppress a smile, and she put her hand out for her piece of mail. "I think that would be a bit extreme."

"But *very* convenient." He tapped the edge of the envelope against his palm before smiling at Jade's sister and clarifying, "For the mail carrier, that is."

Mariah's eyes twinkled with delight. "Of course."

Jade wiggled her fingers and cleared her throat. "My mail?"

He slid the envelope against her palm, but when her

fingers curled around the edge and gently pulled, he didn't let go. Her gaze shot to his, the green depths darkening in awareness.

Ah, sweetheart, you don't stand a chance at resisting what's between us.

The fantasy he'd just read was fresh in his mind, prompting him to issue his boldest challenge to date. "Meet me for a moonlight swim tonight at the pool?"

A startled look passed over her features, then just as quickly she regained her composure. "I think a cold shower would do you more good."

A deep chuckle rumbled in his chest. "Don't doubt that for a minute, Jade."

His blatant admission caught Jade off guard. Her face flushed, and this time when she tugged on her envelope, he released it. It wasn't often he flustered Jade and guessed it was because her sister was witness to their conversation.

He pressed his advantage. "How about at midnight?"

"How about never?" she countered, her impudence restored.

His gaze dropped to that soft, smart mouth of hers. A slow heat licked through his veins and spiraled low. He dallied over those lips, wondering, not for the first time, what her mouth tasted like. He imagined rich honey, warm from the heat of her passion.

"You can't blame a guy for asking," he said, his voice a low, husky timbre. "You never know when a lady might say yes."

"Maybe in another lifetime?" she suggested.

He smiled, undeterred, and picked up his box of books and the treasure that would, before long, have her softening to him and their attraction. "Well, if you change your mind in this lifetime, just let me know."

2

JADE WATCHED KYLE walk away, trying to ignore the breathless sensation swirling within her. There'd been something different in his dark blue eyes today, and in the way he'd watched her—a perceptive awareness, as if he'd known her innermost thoughts and secrets and wanted to fulfill every one of them. Including a moonlight swim.

She shivered, despite the heat of the summer day. He was a big man, lean, fit, with more sex appeal than should have been deemed legal. A white cotton shirt with a popular beer slogan emblazoned on the backside emphasized the width of his shoulders and tapered into the waistband of faded, snug jeans that hugged a great ass and outlined strong thighs. His hips were narrow, his slow, I've-got-all-the-time-in-the-world stride a little cocky and a whole lot self-assured. Much like those charming, heart-stopping smiles of his.

As he turned to enter the complex, she caught a glimpse of the U.S. Marine Corps tattoo on his left arm, just below the cuff of his T-shirt. A souvenir from time spent in the service, she guessed. That piqued her interest, because he didn't seem the type to conform to any rules except his own.

Mariah nodded her head toward Kyle's retreating form. "Kyle *Stephens*, huh?" she said, amusement in her voice. "For real?"

"Every inch," Jade replied flippantly, though there was

nothing light about the warm, shivery, needy way Kyle made her feel inside. He made her think about taking chances and forgetting lessons learned.

Mariah grinned and sighed. "Yeah, it is kind of hard not to notice a body like that one."

Jade choked on incredulous laughter. "Hey, you've got your own great body at home to admire."

Mariah's brows rose. "So leave yours alone?"

"He's not mine," she said succinctly while putting the money Kyle had given her into her cash box.

"Sounds like he's more than willing to be." Mariah bent down to tend to Kayla, giving her one of her favorite squeak toys to play with. When Jade offered no response, she glanced up and asked the million dollar question. "What's going on between you two, anyway? He seemed *awfully* friendly."

"Other than a platonic rendezvous in the lobby to exchange mixed-up mail, nothing."

"Umm-hmm," was Mariah's dubious reply.

Ignoring her sister, Jade turned toward a woman asking the price of a lamp. Using the distraction to her advantage, she involved herself in the task of wheeling and dealing, as much to sell all her unwanted furnishings and knickknacks as to escape her sister's mild interrogation.

The rush of yard-sale shoppers dissipated, leaving Jade alone with Mariah until the next wave of buyers. Reluctantly she made her way back to their shady spot. Settling herself into the folding beach chair next to her sister's, she rummaged through the small cooler they'd brought outside and withdrew a cold soda. Mariah picked up a fussy Kayla and reached for her bottle of apple juice, then gave it to her squirming daughter.

Once Kayla had quieted, Mariah cast a sideways glance

at Jade. "So, are you going to meet him tonight for that moonlight swim?"

Cursing her sister's persistence, and Kyle's tempting offer, Jade took a long drink of her soda. "He wasn't serious, Riah. Kyle is a big flirt, nothing more."

"Oh, I don't know," she said, her tone reflective. "He sounded pretty serious to me. You're the one being difficult." Mariah sighed. "The problem is, you don't even date."

Jade watched a butterfly flutter over a nearby patch of flowers. "Don't worry about me, Riah, I'm just waiting for the right guy to come along." The hard part was, she'd thought she'd found Mr. Right...until she'd realized just how very wrong she'd been. How blind she'd been.

"I am worried about you. How can you expect to find Mr. Right when you keep comparing every guy to Adam?"

Jade's stomach knotted at the mention of the man who'd destroyed her self-esteem and her trust in men's motives. "I'm over Adam. Have been since I told him to go to hell three years ago."

"Oh, I don't doubt that," she said with a quirky little smile. "But he's left you with, well, a lot of emotional scars."

Jade opened her mouth to issue a defensive answer, but Mariah held up a hand, cutting off the same old excuses Jade always fabricated.

"You don't date, and any man who seems the least bit interested you turn down—like this guy," she said in a gentle but firm tone. "You both could have a lot in common."

Her sister was ever the optimist, especially about the male gender. About the only thing she and Kyle Stephens had in common was a similar last name and a tattoo, though hers was less visible and more feminine. She wondered if he'd gotten his as an act of rebellion, too, and smiled despite herself.

"How many women do you think Kyle comes on to like that in a day's time?" Jade mused aloud.

"He seemed sincere, if not a little sure of himself, but you won't even give him a chance." Mariah shook her head in exasperation and glanced heavenward, as if requesting divine intervention with her stubborn sister. "You haven't dated *anyone* since Adam."

"I like my life the way it is. Uncomplicated." Jade studied the bright pink polish on her nails. "I come and go as I please, I buy whatever I please, I dress as I please, and the best part is that I don't have to answer to anyone." Never again would she let a man stifle her identity.

A tiny frown creased Mariah's brows. "Don't you ever feel...lonely?"

"No." A big fat lie—one she kept hoping she'd one day believe. The craving for companionship usually struck her in the evening, when she was sitting in her living room watching TV by herself, or when she slipped into bed at night and the cool satin sheets teased her senses. As she lay awake, unable to sleep, the longing would steal over her, making her yearn to feel warm hands worship her body and ease the ache deep inside. She'd close her eyes and think of *him*...and lose herself in a delicious, satisfying fantasy, where nothing was forbidden and her imagination set the limit.

"Why should I feel lonely?" she said, dismissing her private train of thought. "I've spent the past three years helping to build a good reputation for our interior design firm. Casual Elegance keeps me so busy I hardly have time to think about men and relationships. And when I feel the need to mingle with people and friends, I spend a few hours at Roxy's. That usually kills any desire I might have for male companionship."

"I can see why," Mariah said dryly, having had her own experience with the overzealous men at Roxy's. "Ever think that maybe you're hanging out in the wrong places?"

For all the right reasons, Jade thought, finishing her soda. The men at Roxy's made it easy for her to keep them at a distance, and to remain chaste. Most of them were insensitive, arrogant jerks looking for a one-night stand. She had a few male friends she enjoyed talking to when she frequented the popular nightclub, but she always left alone—not for lack of offers.

Mariah reached for a light blanket and laid it over Kayla, who'd fallen asleep in her arms. When she glanced back at Jade her gaze was shrewd. "You'll never meet a nice, decent guy at Roxy's."

"And you think Kyle Stephens is nice and decent?" Her voice rose incredulously. "He came on to me in front of you, Riah."

"So he's a flirt," Mariah said, defending Kyle's behavior. "Grey's a flirt. All men flirt when they're interested. It's a compliment, not the offense you make it out to be. I don't know what going out with him could hurt."

The gleam in her sister's eyes made her uneasy. "No way are you setting me up, so don't even think it," she said, remembering too well that she'd set Mariah up once, when she and Grey had split up—with disastrous results. Jade was discovering she didn't like being on the receiving end of the ploy. "Just because you're experiencing wedded bliss doesn't mean I'm interested in the same."

Mariah's shoulders sagged in defeat. "What about a family?"

"What about it?"

"Don't you want one?"

"I have one," Jade replied, deliberately misconstruing Mariah's meaning. "I've got great parents, that is when Dad's not nagging at me to settle down, get married and start a family. Sort of like what you're doing right now." She flashed her sister a sassy smile, lightening the moment. "I have you and Grey. And, of course, my favorite niece," she added with affection.

Kayla chose that moment to snuggle into her mother and let out a contented sigh. The sweet, peaceful sound whispered through Jade, tugging at maternal emotions she would have sworn didn't exist in her. If she ignored them, maybe they'd go away.

Mariah grew serious. "I guess I just want you to be as happy as I am."

"I'm happy." She produced a bright smile, albeit a fake one. "See?"

As always, Mariah saw through her act. "And I don't like the thought of you being alone."

"Then you never should have married Grey and moved out of the condo," she joked, and stood when a car pulled up to the curb. Two elderly women got out of the vehicle and ambled toward the items still up for sale.

Blessing the interruption, Jade glanced back at Mariah, intent on putting an end to their conversation. "Seriously, Riah, I'm a big girl, so stop worrying about me."

Before her sister could lecture her further she headed toward the women and greeted them with a cheerful hello. The thought of growing old alone didn't appeal to her, but letting another man close enough to manipulate her feelings and control her life wasn't an option, either.

That's why she'd created her own fantasy man. Because in her experience, fantasies were better than reality.

IN KYLE'S ESTIMATION reality could be much better than fantasy, given the right set of circumstances. And he seemed to have them, in the form of Jade's journal filled with intimate, secret thoughts and fantasies.

Setting his pencil in the crease of the accounting ledger spread open on the desk in front of him, he leaned back in his office chair and thought about the burgundy bound book in his possession. Now that he'd had a few hours to think about his actions earlier that afternoon, he experienced a slight twinge of guilt. A part of his subconscious nagged that if he was a gentleman, he'd give her back the journal. Chivalry had its place, he conceded, but this wasn't the time to be virtuous. Not if he wanted to see if the chemistry between him and Jade was just a spark that would fizzle, or a spark that could spread like wildfire.

And that journal linked them in an intimate way that nothing else could come close to matching.

His plan was definitely reckless, but he'd always lived life on the edge. He'd spent the past few years working hard, then opening The Black Sheep and giving it everything he had to make it a success. During that time he'd dated his share of women. Nothing serious, but then none of those women had interested him beyond a few evenings in their company. The catch had been too effortless, their surrender too willing and easy. No spark. No thrill. And certainly no reason to continue the pursuit when everything was offered so freely.

That's where Jade was different. Though he was attracted to her—she was too sensual of a creature not to stir his libido—it was on more levels than just a physical one. There was something soft and feminine about her. A fascinating blend of vulnerability and sweetness, though she did her best to hide it from anyone who tried to scratch past the surface. It was the woman beneath those intriguing layers that appealed to him and made him wonder what she was *really* like. Made him wonder about those provocative fantasies she wrote.

For six months she'd managed to thrill and excite him. For six months she'd rejected his flirtatious advances and dinner and date invitations. He wasn't about to give up the one thing that gave him the ability to discover the many facets of Jade.

He glanced at his wristwatch. 11:10 p.m. He smiled, wondering if she'd dare to take that midnight swim. She'd been all prim and proper when he'd issued the challenge, but something told him that had been more for her sister's benefit than his.

And he wasn't about to leave anything to chance.

Closing his accounting ledger, he put it away then grabbed his keys from the corner of his desk. He walked out of his office and into the lounge area where his bartender was helping one of the waitresses clear off a recently vacated table. The earlier crowds had dissipated, though the regulars who usually shut down the place were still present.

"Do you mind closing up tonight, Bruce?" Kyle asked. The other man had become a trusted employee and had his own set of keys to the place.

"Not at all, boss," he said with a congenial grin. "Have a good evening."

Kyle grinned right back and headed for the front door. "Oh, I plan to."

BLOWING OUT A FRUSTRATED stream of breath, Jade closed her sapphire blue journal with a snap and gave up on the fantasy she'd been attempting to write. All she'd wanted was to escape and indulge in a private, romantic interlude—the kind she inexorably lost herself in, becoming one with the fantasy she wove.

Her wish wasn't to be.

All she could think about was a moonlight swim. But not with her imagined lover. Someone else had invaded that particular fantasy, someone with features that were unnervingly similar to those of her fantasy lover, but whose wicked smile and smoldering blue eyes were no illusion. Kyle was all too real, possessing a blatant male sensuality that seemed to come as naturally as breathing, and that left her with an aching, yearning feeling after every encounter with him.

And that sensation was something no fantasy lover could compete with.

Cursing Kyle Stephens's gorgeous head and this crazy weakness she seemed to have for him, she put her journal on the nightstand and slid from her new four-poster bed. She padded through her shadowed bedroom to the open sliding doors leading to her balcony, pushed aside the cream-hued sheers in front of the screen, and gazed out across the landscaped courtyard of palm trees and shrubs that separated her wing of condos from half a dozen other units.

And Kyle's condo.

She knew exactly which one was his, and even with only a crescent moon to illuminate the way, she zeroed in on his bedroom balcony, which was dark and currently vacant, along with the rest of the condos. He'd caught her a few times while she'd been watering the plants out on her own terrace, and hadn't had any qualms about flirting with her from across the courtyard, while other residents watched the amusing exchange.

A smile touched her mouth. It was hard not to like someone as playful and easygoing as Kyle. It was even more difficult to keep from giving in to the impulse to go out with him. She knew. She'd been fighting that particular temptation for six months.

She'd lied to her sister that afternoon about not being interested in Kyle. In the light of day it had been easy to lie to herself. Now that she was alone in her big, quiet bedroom with a journal full of fantasies for company, there was no denying the truth.

She was attracted to Kyle Stephens, with an intensity that frightened her because it went beyond anything she'd ever experienced. More and more lately, the wanting consumed her thoughts, teased her senses and enticed her to be a little reckless and wild.

She'd rebelled plenty since her breakup with Adam, but her defiance had been personal, a way to prove to herself that her choices were her own, and that she'd never let another man mold her into something she wasn't.

But beneath the flair, sass and bright and sexy clothes, there was a woman who was still vulnerable. A woman who didn't trust her judgment when it came to men and relationships. A woman scared of falling so hard and fast for a man that she'd do anything to please him, as she had with Adam. It was safer to avoid any kind of emotional involvement and stick to her fantasies.

Her fantasies had been sacred, a way to safely escape from reality...until Kyle's offhanded comment today.

Meet me for a moonlight swim tonight.

She was certain he'd just been teasing and meant nothing more by the suggestion than to use it as an excuse to flirt and ruffle her composure.

It had worked.

Feeling restless, she opened the screen door and stepped out onto the terrace. The terra-cotta tiles were cool beneath her bare feet, a welcome contrast to the sultry summer night. The fluttering hem of her hot pink, silk chemise whispered around her thighs as she walked up to the rod-iron railing. She was acutely aware of the sensuous material sliding across her belly and the tips of her breasts, teasing her like a lover's playful touch. And when she closed her eyes, it was Kyle's hands she imagined.

How about at midnight?

Biting her bottom lip in indecision, she glanced over her shoulder. The digital clock on her nightstand glowed 11:48 p.m. A moonlight swim sounded deliciously decadent on such a warm night, and chances were Kyle was at work, in bed or had found someone else more willing than she.

Reckless. Wild. Undisciplined. For three years she'd written about such behavior. Now she wanted to experience it.

IT WAS A PERFECT NIGHT for a moonlight swim, and he wasn't there. Relief mingled with a disappointment Jade hated to admit to feeling and refused to analyze.

She slipped through the gate surrounding the shimmering pool and recreation building, which housed a game room, a small reception hall for parties, a sauna and a private gym. The exclusive amenities were for resident's use until 10:00 p.m. nightly, unless a later hour was requested for a party or some other occasion.

Tonight, except for the cast of silver moonlight, all was dark and quiet.

Dropping her towel on a lounge chair, she stepped out of her sandals and stripped off the cover-up she'd thrown over her one-piece swimming suit. Without testing the water, she dove into the pool. The water was cool and refreshing, and as she made quiet laps from one end of the pool to another, her body adjusted to the temperature.

Water sluiced over her limbs, like a languid, silken, head-to-toe caress. Feeling uninhibited and a touch on the wild side, she basked in the luxurious sensation, and the sleek, smooth way her skin felt when she brushed her fingers over her arms, across her thighs.

Her fantasy was heaven. The only thing missing was her imagined lover.

She came up for air at the shallow end, and her body jerked in fear at the figure crouched at the edge of the pool where she'd surfaced. Alarm seized her, stifling the scream that would have erupted had her heart not been jammed in her throat.

"I knew you'd come," the intruder said.

Hearing the deep timbre of Kyle's voice, and recognizing those broad shoulders and that dark golden hair cast in moonlight, her terror subsided into anger. "You scared me to death!" she said in a low, furious hiss of breath. Feeling naked and exposed, as if he'd known what she'd been thinking moments before, she backed up, sinking lower into the water, until it lapped around her shoulders and covered the taut peaks of her breasts. "What are you doing here?"

His bad-boy smile was hard to miss, even in the shadows. "I invited you, remember?"

She frowned at his choice of words, so hauntingly familiar. "I thought..." Her sentence trailed off as he straightened, pulled his shirt over his head in one smooth, fluid motion, and tossed it aside.

"You thought what?" His voice was as mesmerizing as the fingers slowly unbuckling the belt at his waist. He popped the snap on his jeans, stealing the coherent reply she'd been about to utter. "That I was joking?" He unzipped the fly of his pants, the erotic sound rasping across her nerve endings and heightening her awareness of the fact that they were alone. "That I wouldn't come?"

Her pulse raced as he hooked his thumbs into the waistband of his jeans. "Both, I guess," she managed to say. "I didn't think you were serious."

"When it comes to you and me, I'm *very* serious." So serious that when he began inching the denim over his hips, the sinful gleam in his eyes dared her to watch.

He was shameless. If he was brazen enough to undress in front of her, then she was going to be just as bold and watch.

He met her challenge, and with all the lazy, practiced ease of a male stripper, he gyrated his hips and shimmied the jeans down his thighs. The only thing missing from his act was a G-string. Instead, he wore striped boxer shorts. The single article of clothing saved her quickly evaporating sanity.

His feet were bare, and he stepped out of the denim and dropped the pants on top of his shirt, then turned toward her again. His chest was as wide as she'd thought, and powerful looking. A light sprinkling of golden hair swirled around flat, brown nipples and arrowed down a lean torso and belly. His waist was trim, his body hard and honed, but not overly muscular.

He was masculine perfection. *He was everything she'd ever dreamed of in a man, a breath-stealing combination of sin and sensuality.*

Oh, Lord, where had that thought come from?

"More?" he asked. His fingers snapped the elastic band of his shorts, drawing her attention to the only part of him he hadn't bared, but seemed more than willing to.

He was so bad, and he knew it, too.

Knowing all it would take was the slightest look or word to give him the incentive he waited for, she chose to change the subject. "I didn't accept your invitation, so why did you bother to show up?"

"You're proof that wishful thinking counts for something." He strolled to the pool's steps and casually descended, making the water ripple toward her in tiny silver-tipped crests. "Since you refused my invitation, what made *you* come?"

A fantasy. One that had somehow become tangled with reality, more and more with each passing second.

He continued advancing, a sensual creature staking a claim. Her stomach tightened in anticipation and apprehension. The game threatened her senses, mocking every lecture she'd ever given herself on the repercussions of getting involved with an aggressive, too confident man.

Before he could touch her, and before her better judgment totally deserted her, she sank below the water and kicked off the bottom toward the deep end. She didn't surface until her palm flattened against the other side of the pool.

Kyle was nowhere to be found. The water looked murky and dark, and she searched for a rippling along the surface, a shadow, anything to indicate Kyle's location. He popped up ten feet away, found her, and disappeared beneath the water again.

Heart pounding, and not knowing what he intended, she headed toward the shallow end in an attempt to elude him. She played mouse to his cat, trying to outsmart him and anticipate his direction and strategy.

He was a far superior opponent. Calculating her next move. Slowly advancing. Silently circling.

The game turned personal, the stakes her surrender. Without a word she knew it, could feel it in the predatory way he stalked her.

It was a matter of time before he caught her.

He cornered her at the shallow end of the pool. She crouched by the ledge in the direct center while he approached from the middle, leaving his right and left side clear. Knowing she had a fifty-fifty chance of evading him, she gave the impression of feinting to his right, but once she was underwater kicked off the side of the pool to circle around to his left.

She'd barely begun to hope she'd fooled him when strong fingers clamped around her ankle and pulled her backward. Her first instinct was to panic and struggle, but not knowing how deep they were she could only trust the man slowly reeling her in.

Large hands skimmed up her legs, up the sides of her thighs, over the curve of her hips, until he finally anchored an arm around her waist and pulled up. When they broke the surface, she was breathless. Not from lack of oxygen, but from the sleek, slick body pressed so intimately along her back, her bottom, her thighs. Her swimsuit was little protection against the scorching heat he generated.

"Gotcha," he murmured into her ear.

His own heavy breathing touched her neck, and her breasts swelled in response. "Let me go." She gripped his arm and squirmed, but his hold didn't budge.

"You never answered my question," he countered, easing them toward the side of the pool at the shallow end. "What made you come tonight?"

She had no answer, at least not one that made any sense to herself, or one he wouldn't gloat over.

"Was it because of this?"

The hand splayed on her belly slid up and cupped her firm breast in his palm. She gasped in shock, then groaned as his thumb flicked over her nipple. The tip instantly hardened, giving him the answer he sought. *Yes.*

He upped the stakes of the game.

Reaching the edge, he turned her around and boosted her bottom onto the side of the pool. Before she could scramble away, he eased her legs apart with the heel of his hands and stepped between. His long fingers hooked beneath her knees and pulled her toward him until her thighs hugged his hips in a purely sexual manner.

She gasped. He was aroused, hard and throbbing against her. The only thing preventing him from sliding deep within her body was her swimsuit and his boxer shorts.

Her response was hot, liquid and illicit.

A strangled sound rose up in her throat, part thrill, part fear. She could feel herself tumbling, falling…for him. She tried to scoot back, but his hands gripped her hips, forcing her to feel the passion she kindled in him.

"Don't be so shocked, Jade," he said, his tender smile at odds with his body's fierce need. "This is what you do to me. You turn me on, physically and mentally. I've never made a secret of wanting you, but now you've found out for yourself."

Yes, now she knew. And she'd never be able to forget.

Her fingers curled around the ledge, to keep from touching his chest, gleaming with droplets of water. She stared into his eyes, as dark as the velvet night sky above. That familiar ache started within her, the wanting…

"Kyle…"

His thumbs slipped beneath the elastic band of her swimsuit where it cut high on her hips. "Leopard skin, hmm?" he said of the print on her suit, obviously not interested in her feeble protests. "If I peel this away, will I find a tiger beneath?"

There *was* something just a little untamed happening inside her.

"Or maybe a sweet little kitty cat?" Leaning forward, he lapped the water drops from her throat, his tongue soft and warm as it tasted her skin.

She quivered and all but curled into him and purred.

"Which one would it be?" he mused, his lips lingering at a sensitive spot just below her ear. "Tiger or kitten?"

"Both felines have claws," she said, cursing the breathless quality of her voice, which diminished the brassy retort she'd been striving for.

"That they do," he agreed, chuckling. "But if they're petted and stroked the right way, they usually become docile and compliant." As if to prove his point, he swept a hand down her spine, smoothing his palm over the wet, slippery suit that clung like skin. "I want to stroke you." That same hand passed over her hip and slid down her thigh to her knee, the caress electrifying her nerves. "I want to pet you."

She caught the groan rising in her throat, but there was nothing she could do to prevent the softening of her body, the yearning spiraling deep inside, the need to succumb to the desire singeing her senses. What he was suggesting was wicked, erotic and lascivious.

And she wanted to experience it.

Shrouded in darkness, spellbound by the hunger and promises gleaming in his eyes, her inhibition fled. In its place was a wildness she'd only imagined and wrote about, an uncontrollable urge to give in to the lush, decadent sensations of her fantasies.

"Close your eyes, sweetheart," he murmured, lowering his head to nuzzle his soft, warm lips along her neck. "And feel the heat between us...."

Moaning in acquiescence, she let her lashes fall and her body respond. He lifted his hands from her knees and tangled his fingers in her damp hair, using his hold to tilt her head back and give his marauding mouth better access to her throat.

He nibbled her neck, his teeth grazing her skin, his tongue sliding, swirling, from her earlobe to the base of her throat. Jade's grip on the ledge of the pool tightened, and she welcomed the distraction of the concrete scraping into her palms.

Which lasted all of three seconds. He ruthlessly bombarded her senses, shattering her defenses with the slow slide of his hands along her neck to her shoulders, the wet heat of his mouth gliding along her flesh, the incredible softness of his tongue...a tongue that was currently licking droplets of water from her skin in long, languid laps.

Like a big cat enjoying a bowl of rich cream.

"Kyle..." Her voice quivered, and so did her belly, her thighs. She was strung too tight.

He pushed the straps of her suit from her shoulders, letting them fall down her arms. The wet spandex clung to her breasts, and she gulped huge breaths as he rained soft kisses on her chest and his tongue stroked over the full, straining swells of her breasts.

Fire. His touch was pure flame, burning her up from the inside out. He'd yet to touch or kiss her intimately, in all the places she ached, though she felt as though he'd branded her in every elemental way. He'd seduced her mind, her body, her soul. The earthy masculine scent of him filled her head, making her dizzy with a need that went beyond the physical.

She struggled to clear her mind of the desire making her weak, the desire making her want a man who wielded way too much power over her body and emotions. She silently cursed, angry at him for making her feel things she'd kept hidden for three years, and furious at her body's traitorous response to his caresses. Dammit, she wanted Kyle Stephens, but she didn't want to want him. Wanting him was dangerous. Wanting him made her vulnerable.

And she refused to be susceptible to any man ever again.

Feeling trapped and as if the situation was slipping beyond her control, she pressed her hands against his shoulders and gave a distinct push. The sudden move caught him off guard and he stumbled back a step, giving her enough room to slip off the side of the pool and into the water. With a deep breath of air, she dove beneath the surface and headed toward the deep end, away from him.

When her lungs finally demanded oxygen and she came up for air, Kyle wasn't where she'd left him. Her eyes searched the darkness, and her pulse raced at the thought of him beneath the water, hunting for her. She waited, listening, watching.

He was gone. She realized that much when she finally noticed his clothes were no longer where he'd left them.

She shivered, the chill settling deep. The only indication that she hadn't imagined the whole tryst was the trail of wet footprints leading out the gate.

3

SHE COULDN'T AVOID the inevitable any longer.

Jade finished changing from the culotte outfit she'd worn that day at the office to a pair of comfortable violet-and-pink plaid leggings and a purple silk tank top. Kyle was home; she'd seen his Jeep when she'd parked her car. And she had a piece of his mail she'd been holding onto for two days. Considering their mailboxes didn't have convenient slots to drop misdelivered mail into, she was obligated to hand deliver this letter herself.

She hadn't seen him in four days, ever since the surreal night at the pool when he'd seduced her, then disappeared, leaving her bereft and bewildered by the whole scenario. She had to admit, at least to herself, that avoiding him was deliberate and planned on her part, though she was never certain what Kyle's strategy might be. He was a master at catching her off-guard, when she least expected to see him.

Their day and night schedules had conflicted over the past few days, enough to keep them missing one another in the lobby, and it seemed Kyle was spending more time out than in, arriving home after midnight. That she noticed when his lights went on in his condo irritated her. One night, she'd sat out on her darkened balcony and watched his silhouette through the thin curtains of his sliding door as he'd moved around his bedroom and stripped off his clothes.

Her heart pounded at the memory, at the way her body had warmed in an instinctive, feminine way. It was crazy. He'd been clear across the courtyard and oblivious to her harmless voyeurism, but now she knew exactly what Kyle was capable of doing to her senses, her body. Her imagination had taken over from there, creating a fantasy that fulfilled the ache deep within her.

There wasn't much she could do about the loneliness that came in the aftermath.

Slipping into a pair of espadrilles, she exited her bedroom, determined to leave her private thoughts there as well, where they belonged. Picking up Kyle's mail from her glass-topped dinette table, and grabbing her house keys from the counter, she headed toward the other side of the complex.

Interestingly enough, the return address was from a Christy Stephens in Detroit, Michigan, which piqued her curiosity, making her wonder who this mystery woman was. Sister? Mother? Ex-wife? She realized she didn't know much about Kyle's personal life other than the fact that he owned The Black Sheep bar, but then she'd never allowed their relationship to extend beyond acquaintance.

Until she'd gone for a moonlight swim. That night they'd been intimate in a way that made familiar seem tame and boring. He'd gotten under her skin, touched the part of her soul hungry for a man's touch. It was as if he'd known what she wanted, what she needed....

But the emotional risk of accepting what Kyle offered was too destructive, as she well knew. She could fall hard and deep for Kyle Stephens and his playful, sometimes reckless behavior, but it was his unflappable confidence and assertive nature that threatened her own confidence, and her judgment.

Determined to take a giant step back to secure those boundaries he'd so boldly crossed, Jade knocked on his door. After what had transpired between them, it was impossible to think they could revert back to mere acquaintances, but she'd settle for being friends. Friends she could handle. Friends didn't try and dictate your life and make unnecessary demands on your time.

When a minute passed and no one answered the door, she rang the doorbell. Again she waited, then knocked louder, debating on slipping the letter under the door. She bent to do just that when the door opened and she found herself staring at bare feet. Slowly she straightened.

She'd obviously caught Kyle fresh out of the shower, and considered herself lucky that he'd at least thrown on a pair of black jeans instead of greeting her in a towel wrapped around his hips. Droplets of water still clung to his defined and muscular chest. He stopped towel-drying his damp, shaggy hair and pushed the unruly strands away from his face with his fingers. Unabashed pleasure lit his sapphire blue eyes, along with an intimate knowledge that made her blood thrum heavily in her veins.

It didn't take much to guess he was thinking about their moonlight swim, and how he'd nearly made her come undone.

She was determined not to go that route with him. "Did I catch you at a bad time?" she asked.

"For you, it's never a bad time." Draping the towel around his neck, he leaned his shoulder against the door frame, which he nearly filled. His gaze did a slow, sweeping appraisal, generating a fever-warm sensation just beneath the surface of her skin. When his eyes met hers again, the depths were filled with a playful charm and a potent heat. "Unless you want it to be," he added with a reckless grin. "And in that case I'd be happy to oblige."

She didn't doubt he'd give her a "bad" time, with satisfaction being the ultimate goal. "I'm sorry to disappoint you, but my visit is going to be short and brief—"

Her words died on her lips and her thoughts fled when he reached out and slid his fingers through the layered hair at the side of her face, his touch infinitely gentle. His brows lifted in bemusement as his gaze flickered over her hair, then to her eyes. Her pulse leapt, but she didn't pull away.

"You colored your hair," he mused, testing the silk and texture of the strands between his fingers. "And it's shorter and styled differently."

The man didn't miss a thing. The color was a muted auburn that complimented her skin tone, and her hair had been cut into a soft, tousled style that her stylist, Pierre, had assured her looked chic and classy. "I had it done a few days ago."

And as she'd sat in the salon chair with the chemicals turning her golden brown hair into a soft cinnamon hue, she'd realized just how badly the episode at the pool with Kyle had rattled her. Her spur-of-the-moment decision to change her hair color and style had been a compulsive need to reassure herself she was still in control of herself as an individual. She recognized the symptom, a subtle act of rebellion to make sure no man made the mistake of thinking he could change her, or mold her into something she wasn't ever again.

Including Kyle Stephens.

He tilted his head, as if to scrutinize her from another angle. His gaze pierced hers, making her feel as though he could see straight to her soul and was probing all her secrets. It was a disturbing sensation.

"Who is the real Jade?" he murmured, gliding his thumb along her jaw to her chin.

Only she knew, and she preferred to keep it that way. "I'm not sure I know what you mean," she said in a vague, dismissive way.

"Oh, I'm sure you do," he countered, seeing past her aloofness. "I like the new haircut and color, sweetheart, but it doesn't change the person inside." Before she could formulate a response to that stunningly insightful remark, he stepped back and cleared the way for her to enter his condo. "Why don't you come in and we'll discuss this short, brief visit of yours?"

She hesitated, knowing business between them could be conducted in a matter of seconds from where she stood. But there was that subtle dare in his eyes that provoked her rebellious nature, made her want to prove that she could be in the same room with him yet maintain her emotional distance.

She stepped inside, and he closed the door, and she was immediately enveloped by the warm, masculine scents pervading the room. Heat and musk. Leather and wood, scents which reflected his choice of furnishings.

"So, to what do I owe this pleasure?"

The word *pleasure* rolled off his tongue like a caress to her senses, making her remember the night at the pool, which was beginning to seem like a distant dream. Or another one of her unbridled fantasies. He'd yet to mention the incident, which made her wonder if her imagination *had* gone a little wild that evening, creating an erotic fantasy that had seemed real, but in fact had only been an illusion.

Unwilling to ponder that unsettling thought any further, she handed him the envelope. "I got a letter addressed to you."

He took the letter without looking at it, feigning disappointment. "And here I was hoping you'd stopped by because you'd missed me."

She smiled and gathered up some much needed sass. "I know it must be a blow to that enormous ego of yours, but out of sight puts you out of mind."

He laughed, that giant ego unwounded by her words. "Then I'll have to do something to remedy that."

She didn't doubt that he would.

Pulling the towel from around his neck, he draped it over the back of a barstool at the kitchen counter, then strolled into the adjoining living room. She casually followed him deeper into his bachelor domain, keeping her distance, while the decorator in her absorbed his understated, comfortable furnishings.

Standing next to the chocolate-colored leather couch, Kyle ripped open the flap of the envelope and withdrew the correspondence within, all the while aware of the woman in his condo. Acutely so, considering she'd brought with her the faint scent of peaches, which was quickly becoming an aphrodisiac. That she'd actually stepped through the threshold was a wonder, and he wasn't about to scare her off by crowding her.

She expected him to take advantage of her being in his territory; he could see the wariness in her eyes, despite her sass. And the little tiger was out to prove she wasn't intimidated by their close, private proximity. Physically she was safe, but he had no reservations about arousing her mentally, which he'd done at the door.

She was waiting for him to mention their moonlight swim and gloat about her open, eager response to him. But he had no intention of breaking the spell of that magical, sensual night by dragging it out in the open and baring her deepest secrets. He'd given her her fantasy, and in return he'd been the one seduced by her sweetness and vulnerability, though he'd bet The Black Sheep that she'd never verbally admit to such a weakness. He saw her caution and reserve for what it was, but it didn't deter him. Jade had become a fever that constantly burned through his veins. Not one of the women he'd had over the years had ever come close to stimulating him beyond a sexual level.

Beyond a doubt, Jade aroused him sexually, but the added bonus of being matched intellectually was just as exhilarating, if not more so. Sparring with her was like foreplay, a seduction of senses, a slow building of sexual tension, a little naughty and damned exciting.

Returning his attention to the correspondence, he unfolded the handwritten letter, surprised when half a dozen snapshots that had been enclosed fluttered to the floor. That's what he got for paying more attention to Jade than what he was doing.

The pictures went in six different directions, and while he bent to gather the ones by his feet, Jade picked up two that had drifted her way. She glanced at the snapshots of a young woman, then handed them back to him.

Curiosity warmed her eyes to an intriguing shade of violet. "Is that your sister?"

He grinned at her wrong assumption. "No, it's my daughter, Christy."

Her eyes rounded in astonishment. "You have a daughter *that* old?"

"Yep." Mouth crooking in a fond smile, he gazed at a recent snapshot of Christy, who looked the spitting image of her mother, with golden blond hair, brown eyes and a smile destined to break a lot of hearts. He sighed deeply, and somewhat regretfully, for all the years lost. "A just-turned-seventeen-year-old, boy-crazy, I-need-a-car-Dad, kind of daughter."

She scrutinized his face. "You don't look old enough to have a seventeen-year-old daughter."

He knew she was mentally counting backward, trying to match his current age with how old he would have been when his daughter had been born. "I'm hitting the downhill slide of thirty-five," he said, and before she had a chance to do any more quick mental math, he added, "Christy was born when I was eighteen."

She looked taken aback, and even more inquisitive than before. "That seems awfully young to start a family."

"It is," he admitted, especially considering how close his own daughter was to that tender young age. "Unfortunately, at that age I wasn't thinking much with my brain but that other part of my anatomy dictated by raging hormones. Christy is a result of a brief summer fling I had after graduating high school."

Jade moved to the oak wall unit and examined the other pictures he'd framed and set out. "Does she live with her mother?"

"Yeah, back in Detroit." After tucking the recent photos and letters back into the envelope, he set the correspondence on the coffee table. He always enjoyed reading his daughter's letters; they were always full of amusing anecdotes about her life that made him smile, sometimes laugh out loud. They'd established a healthy friendship over the years, one that had become a precious treasure to him.

She glanced over her shoulder at him. "That's quite a ways from California."

And there were times when he felt every one of the miles that separated him from the two families he'd never really been a part of. "That's where I'm from, and Christy's mother, too." He came up beside her and pointed to a framed photograph of his daughter standing between two adults. "That's Christy's mom, Jamie Ann, and her stepfather, Tony."

Jade gaped incredulously. "You framed a picture of your ex-wife *and* her husband?"

He knew how odd that sounded, considering most severed relationships weren't so amicable. But Jamie Ann had been one of the few people who'd understood his reckless nature and hadn't tried to put a tether on it, or him. For that alone, he would always care deeply for her. "She's not my ex-wife," he said. "And the three of us are all really good friends."

He could tell the triangle boggled Jade's mind, and was aware his comment informed her he hadn't "done the responsible thing" and married Jamie Ann. But there was so much more to the story than met the eye, so much history to wade through, history that had motivated the rash actions of the eighteen-year-old hellion he'd been.

Instead of pursuing something so personal, she gave him an easygoing smile. "You're not very traditional, are you?"

"'Fraid I never have been," he drawled, returning her smile with one of his own. "And most likely never will be. Being a bachelor suits me just fine."

"Umm." She went back to studying the snapshots, seemingly digesting that bit of information.

He, too, glanced over the cluster of photographs showing his daughter in various stages of growth, and he experienced a familiar sense of loss. Even though Kyle hadn't married Jamie Ann, he'd fallen in love with Christy the moment Jamie Ann had plopped the squalling two-week-old infant into his arms.

Over the years he saw his daughter at least once a year, talked to her on the phone monthly and wrote regularly, and he hadn't missed one child-support payment—even when times had been tough and it had been a choice between food in his belly or his daughter's welfare.

He didn't delude himself into believing that he was the ideal dad, and the resulting regret he'd experienced as he'd matured into a man was his cross to bear. He might have fathered Christy, but Tony was her dad in the truest sense of the word. Kyle was grateful that his daughter had been raised with love and the guidance of two parents who had her best interests at heart.

"Your daughter looks just like her mom," Jade said, bringing him back from the past.

He met Jade's gaze, liking this easy friendship they were forging. It went hand in hand with the trust he intended to establish, and the attraction he meant to pursue. "She might look like her mom," he said with a wry grin, "but trust me when I tell you she's a chip off the old block."

Amusement lit her eyes. "How so?"

"Unfortunately for Jamie Ann, Christy's got my wild, reckless blood." But she demonstrated nothing more than healthy, normal teenage behavior, rash impulses that pushed boundaries but rarely crossed them. Nothing at all like the hostility and resentment that drove him to defy his father at every opportunity, and shock his family and his parents' elite group of friends with his outrageous exploits.

"If you're from Michigan, what brought you to California?" Jade asked.

"Camp Pendleton," he said, naming the military base near San Diego. "I joined the marines three months out of high school, came to California, decided I liked seeing the sun year-round, and never went back."

She eyed his left bicep, her lashes falling half-mast. "So, that tattoo of yours isn't a fake, then?"

He chuckled. "Nope." He turned to glance at his arm, and the indelible reminder of his stint in the service flexed with the movement. "It's a permanent souvenir of one wild, crazy night blurred by tequila."

Her mouth curled at the corners, and her eyes danced with a delightful secret. Then she shook her head and laughed, the sound so pure and sweet it reached him on a gut level and grabbed hard.

He wanted to probe the reason for her amusement, but he'd already spent more time with her than he had to spare at the moment. Reluctantly his gaze strayed to the clock on the wall, then drifted back to her.

He took in her unreserved expression, her affable smile, and knew a moment of supreme satisfaction for having breached her do-not-cross zone. "As much as I've enjoyed talking to you, I've got to be at The Black Sheep in half an hour. I spent the day helping the contractor tear down walls in the new restaurant, and I was just getting cleaned up for my shift tonight when you caught me."

As if realizing how much time she'd spent with him, her eyes widened ever so slightly, and she took a telling step back. "I've got to go anyway. I just wanted to bring you your mail."

"I appreciate the personal delivery service," he said, following her to the door and enjoying the view from behind.

Once outside his condo, she turned and gave him a smile. "Have a good night at work."

"Oh, I will." How could he not after getting closer to Jade in twenty minutes than he had in the past six months? "I'll see ya around." Leaning a shoulder against the frame, he watched her walk down the corridor until she turned the corner at the end. Slipping back inside his condo, he grinned as he headed back to his room to finish dressing.

He'd thrown her a curveball today. Purposely, and with impressive results. She'd arrived stiff as starch and full of preconceived ideas about how he'd behave, and had left relaxed and smiling.

Kyle's grin deepened as he tucked his black T-shirt into his jeans then grabbed the leather belt he'd left at the foot of his bed. He'd flirted—it was a natural part of the chemistry between him and Jade—but he'd also enjoyed talking to her on a casual, getting-to-know-one-another level. And the beauty of it was, in the process, he'd stripped away a layer of defense and smoothed it over with friendship and easy rapport.

Between the journal of fantasies he had in his possession and his slow, gradual persuasion, his little tiger didn't stand a chance.

JADE TURNED HER FLASHY red Mazda Miata—a present to herself three years ago to celebrate her newfound independence—into the driveway leading to her private parking alcove. A horn blared and she glanced in her rearview mirror to find Kyle pulling in behind her.

He drove a navy-colored Jeep with a soft top, which he used only when it was raining. The open-air vehicle framed by thick roll bars and little else suited that rebel attitude of his, and gave truth to his comment about enjoying the California sun year-round.

She waved out her open window and saw him grin before she made the turn to her parking spot and he drove past to his. Once she was parked, she lifted her attaché case and purse from the passenger seat and slid from the low-slung sports car.

They met on the main walkway leading to the lobby of

the complex, though he had to jog a short distance to catch up to her deliberately clipped pace.

"Those heels sure do make your legs look great in that miniskirt," he said once they were side by side. "But it baffles me how a woman can walk so fast and steady in them without toppling over."

"Years of practice." She smiled at him, taking in his wind-tousled hair, shot with strands of gold from the sun, and eyes sparkling with mischief. "If I didn't know better, I'd think you'd planned this."

He didn't look the least bit offended by her suspicion. "Hey, what can I say? I've got great timing. Besides, I've been wanting to talk to you. This saves me a trip to your place."

Despite how much she'd enjoyed talking with Kyle the other night at his condo, she preferred the neutral territory of the lobby to the private, intimate sanctuary of her home.

A tall, curvy blonde exited the front of the complex and sauntered down the walkway toward them, her gaze riveted to Kyle. She wore a tight, skimpy pair of shorts and a workout top that revealed more than it covered. Her mouth lifted in a sultry, come-hither smile, and she tossed her wild mane of hair over her shoulder in a deliberately seductive gesture.

"Hi, Kyle," she said, giving him a thorough once-over that was at once possessive and appreciative. Jade was irritated to realize it struck a resentful chord within her.

"Hello, Lynette," Kyle replied pleasantly.

Jade recognized the woman as a tenant, and guessed that she and Kyle were acquaintances. Or perhaps a whole lot more, Jade speculated, noting the way the blonde was eating him up with her hungry gaze.

"You working tonight?" the other woman asked hopefully.

Kyle grinned. "I'm closing the place down."

Lynette looked pleased. "Count on me being there." She trailed a finger up his arm and along his shoulder as she passed him in that loose-hipped walk of hers, then added, "Save me a place at the bar."

The whole exchange provoked Jade's ire, which grated on her nerves even more because she had no claim to Kyle. Nor did she want one, she told herself firmly. The lecture to herself didn't improve her mood.

"I see you have your own fan club at The Black Sheep," she muttered, unable to hold back the catty remark.

An infuriatingly sexy grin curved his mouth. "Jealous?"

"Of course not!" she denied a little too vehemently. Reaching the double glass doors leading into the lobby, she reached for the handle, but before she could pull, his hand closed over hers, giving her little choice but to stop.

Her pulse leapt, as it always did when he touched her. No man had ever had such an instantaneous, blood-heating effect on her. It unsettled her that Kyle had that much influence over her body and mind.

She jerked her hand away and forced herself to meet his gaze, which she'd fully expected to be brimming with amusement at her obvious negative reaction to the blonde. Instead, she saw only sincerity and a lush, healthy dose of desire. For her.

"You have no reason to be jealous," he said, splaying his hand on the flat surface of the glass door to keep it closed. "I've been faithful to you from the day we first met."

She stared at him, stunned and incredulous, certain he was joking, but the truth of his words was reflected in his dark blue eyes. "That's quite a noble sacrifice, but it's totally unnecessary."

"I don't seem to have a choice in the matter." He sighed with the burden and leaned closer, revealing in a confidential tone, "Charlie isn't attracted to anyone but you."

"Charlie?" She burst out laughing, tickled at the prospect of Kyle, the image of virility and sex appeal, naming that masculine part of his body.

He shrugged without a hint of embarrassment. "He's very particular."

Her mirth subsided. "And you're absolutely crazy."

"Just about you," he said, his deep voice so earnest her heart gave a distinct thump in her chest.

Summoning a defense against Kyle's charm, she gave him a sassy grin. "Don't bother wasting a vow of abstinence on me. The long wait will make you eligible for the monastery."

He lifted a golden brow, and his mouth curved oh-so-enticingly. Daringly. "You willing to put your money where your mouth is, tiger?"

A shiver rippled down her spine. Belatedly, she realized her grave mistake at challenging Kyle—a wholly sexual male who had made it his mission to pursue her.

Knowing he had all that sexual energy stored up for her made her weak in the knees and gave her a sense of power that was more exciting than she cared to admit...but not so exhilarating that she'd accept his outrageous dare.

"I guess not," Kyle said, winning the challenge by default. He opened the glass door and inclined his head for her to precede him.

She slipped past him with a murmured, "Thank you," and they strolled down the carpeted corridor toward the lobby. Remembering something he'd said earlier, before the incident with Lynette had shifted them onto a different course, she asked, "So, what did you want to talk to me about?"

He glanced at her and smiled amiably, as if he hadn't come close to propositioning her minutes before. The man knew how to throw her off-kilter like nobody's business. "How's the decorating business?"

Ah, work she could handle, she thought as they stopped at the bank of mailboxes in the lobby. "Busy."

"Do you have room to take on another client?"

"I never refuse business." Setting down her attaché, she rummaged for her key in her purse, inserted it into the slot and opened the metal box.

"I guarantee it's a sure thing," he drawled as he retrieved his own mail and flipped through the few standard-size envelopes. "A few months ago I bought the building next to my bar. I'm expanding The Black Sheep, and I'm going to need someone to decorate the new restaurant and give the bar a facelift."

She sorted through her own mail, finding everything delivered accurately. "And you want Casual Elegance to do it?"

Stuffing his mail into the back pocket of his jeans, he relocked his box. "No, I want *you* to do it."

She lifted her gaze to his. He sounded and appeared very sure of himself and his decision, despite the fact that he'd never seen her portfolio or scheduled a consultation. Decorators were a different breed, each one with a style and flair all their own. Sometimes her bold and eccentric taste clashed with certain clients' vision and ideas. Those accounts she gladly handed over to Mariah, who was far more traditional and straightforward in her decorating approach.

However, the thought of letting her creative juices run

free with a restaurant and bar was exciting, because it would be a first for Casual Elegance, who specialized in decorating and remodeling plush offices, upscale model houses, and custom-built homes. This project would be a challenging and refreshing change, not to mention an impressive addition to her already fat portfolio.

Tucking her mail into the outside pocket of her attaché, she straightened and faced him, not quite ready to grasp the treasure he dangled in front of her. "Your offer is generous and your faith in my ability is flattering, considering you haven't seen my portfolio and I haven't even given you a preliminary consultation. How do you even know I'm any good?"

Casually propping his hip against the sofa a few feet away, he crossed his arms over his chest and let his gaze flicker over her. His eyes traveled over her emerald green silk blouse, lingering for several heartbeats where the last closed button revealed a swell of cleavage bordered in sheer lace, before he continued down her black pleated miniskirt, and along the length of her legs. Slowly, and with enough heat to spark an internal flash fire, he dragged his eyes back to hers.

"No doubt about it," he said, his low, sexy voice flowing over her like warmed molasses. "I think you're plenty good."

She ignored the double meaning and the flutter of awareness deep in her belly. "I suppose it's your dollar, you can spend it any way you choose."

"You're a smart businesswoman." He grinned and tilted his head. A lock of tawny hair fell over his forehead, making him look like the rascal Jade knew him to be. "So, have you ever been to The Black Sheep?"

"Would it make a difference if I have or haven't?"

"Nope. Just curious."

"No, I've never been there," she said, feeling obligated to make him aware that she was accepting the job as blindly as he offered it. "It's really not my type of place."

"Ummm." The sound he made was thoughtful, as was the way he looked at her. "How do you know that if you've never been there?"

Her face warmed when she realized she'd stereotyped his establishment without grounds. "I've heard about it," she quickly qualified with a shrug. "It's a typical country-western bar. Casual, a little rowdy. Mostly blue-collar clientele."

He didn't refute her description. "And you prefer Roxy's and the more *sophisticated* clientele they have to offer."

She shrugged indifferently, not about to defend her choice of nightclub to him.

"Considering my direct competition seems to be Roxy's, I'd like to upscale." He braced his hands on the sofa on either side of his hips and crossed his legs at the ankle, briefly drawing her attention to the way soft denim encased his muscular thighs, and other parts of his anatomy. "I want to keep the same casual, blue-collar atmosphere, but class up the interior a bit."

Her mind whirled, planning ahead. "When will the restaurant be done?"

"Another four to six weeks should do it."

She nodded, digesting the time frame she had to work with. "Then we want to get started on colors and fabrics and a design to fit your theme."

"I've got a general idea of what I want," he said, a charmingly impish grin creasing the corners of his mouth, "but I was hoping you could help me tie it all together."

"That's what you're gonna pay me to do." She flashed him a quick smile and dug through her purse for her business-card holder. Finding it, she pulled out a cream-colored card with a bright abstract design in the corner beneath Casual Elegance, and her name printed across the middle. She handed it to him. "You can give me a call at the office and we can set up an appointment for an initial consultation to figure out what you want, the cost and to sign a preliminary contract."

He glanced at her business card and flicked the corner with his thumb. When he met her gaze again his eyes glimmered with purpose. "What if an emergency comes up and I need to contact you at home?"

"I don't give out my home phone number to clients." She commended herself on her quick response. She was determined to do the job and maintain a professional relationship with Kyle. "My pager and cell-phone number are on the business card. Do you have a day in mind that's convenient for you and I to meet at the bar?"

His brow creased as he mentally flipped through the upcoming week. "How does next Monday late afternoon sound? Quitting time for the contractors is around three-thirty, so any time after that we'd be able to walk through the restaurant."

"That sounds fine." She dropped her business-card holder back in her purse. "But I'll check my schedule to be sure I'm free and get back to you."

"Great." He straightened and moved closer to where she stood. "Got a pen so I can give you my number?"

Grabbing the one she always kept clipped to the outside pocket of her purse, she handed it to him. He pulled the cap off with his teeth, and she realized at the same moment he stepped toward her that he didn't have a piece of paper.

Judging by the bad-boy gleam in his eyes, she had a wild suspicion he didn't have any intention of using one.

His thighs pinned hers, and the automatic objection that rose in her throat dissolved into a groan as intense body heat and the heady, male scent of him surrounded her. She felt drugged and dizzy, unable to form a coherent word or thought. Before she could react or regain her wits, he deftly unfastened the top button on her blouse, swept the collar aside, and brazenly scrawled his home and work number on the full swell of her breast, right over her racing-out-of-control heart and just above the delicate, sheer lace cupping the mounds of flesh. To her mortification, her nipples grew tight and hard. Achingly so.

Cheeks flaming, she gaped at him, too stunned by his scandalous stunt to get angry. Too shocked by her body's hot, shameless response to his touch to slap his hand away.

When he was done, he lifted his head and casually restored her blouse to order. "Call anytime," he murmured, a wolfish smile claiming his lips, a smile so predatory she knew the pursuit was far from over, no matter how professional *she* planned to be.

He turned and walked away, leaving her standing on shaky legs and fighting a fierce rush of desire she had no defense against.

She wanted Kyle Stephens.

She pressed her palms to her warm cheeks and shuddered in denial. He was dangerous. Threatening all her emotional barriers. Seducing her mind and body with little effort, seemingly knowing just what she wanted. What she needed. Physically and emotionally.

Lord help her, she wasn't sure how much longer she could resist him.

And that knowledge frightened her most of all.

4

The heat of the sun overhead warmed her skin and intensified the scent of the ripe, plump peach her lover held to her lips. Her mouth watered for a taste, and she closed her eyes and licked her lips in anticipation.

"Take a bite," he murmured.

She did, sinking her teeth deep into the lush fruit. A sweet burst of flavor filled her mouth, and she moaned in pleasure before taking another bite. Juice dribbled down her chin, and she lifted her hand to wipe it away.

He reached out and caught her wrist. "Don't. I'll do it for you...when I'm done."

She shivered at the promise in his gaze, and the deliberate way he squeezed the peach in his hand, mashing it into pulp. With his thumb he dug out the pit and flicked it onto the grass. A slow, wicked grin lifted his mouth.

Guessing his intent, she attempted to scramble away. He caught her around the waist and playfully tumbled her onto her back on the soft blanket beneath them. He straddled her waist, pinning her arms to her sides with his muscular thighs.

All play ceased, but that's exactly what she wanted. Her breathing deepened as, slowly, he undid the buttons on the front of her dress and spread the sides open. Unclasping her bra, he pushed that aside as well. Her breasts swelled beneath his dark gaze and her nipples hardened into tight peaks. She arched in subtle invitation.

Obliging her, he smeared the cool, slick pulp over the curves of her breasts, kneading and shaping the plump flesh in his hands before he lowered his body alongside hers and feasted on the fruit. His tongue lapped her breasts in long, languid strokes until finally, his mouth closed over a nipple and suckled deeply.

A sharp gasp caught in her throat and she speared her fingers through his hair, holding him to her breast and twining her legs around his as breathtaking pleasure flooded her limbs and her body softened just for him....

"*CHRIST*." Breathing as though there was a lack of oxygen in the room, Kyle swore again, more bluntly this time, and tossed Jade's journal onto the bed next to where he lay. His body was rock-hard, his mind just as seduced by her fantasy. He scrubbed his hands over his face in frustration and squeezed his eyes shut, trying to banish the images that were sending blood straight toward his groin.

Stupid idea. All he could see was Jade, spread out on a blanket in a meadow, her breasts shimmering from sunlight and peach nectar, and her dress tangled around her thighs, revealing long, slim legs splayed enticingly. And all he could think about was sliding between those thighs, wrapping those incredible legs tight around his waist and burying himself to the hilt. He'd give her more pleasure than she could imagine, and he'd take her places her fantasy lover didn't even know existed—dark, provocative places where inhibitions weren't allowed, and every adventurous thrill and erotic fantasy was fulfilled. *By him.*

He stroked his hand over the thick bulge in his jeans, and groaned deep in his throat. Popping the button, he unzipped his fly to release some of the pressure. Unfortunately only one person could ease the ache. Jade.

Drawing in a deep breath to reduce the tension in his body, he stacked his hands beneath his head and focused his thoughts on something other than sex. Staring at the shadows on the ceiling cast by the lamp on his nightstand, he steered his mind toward another topic: the complex facets of Jade Stevens.

Her fantasies told him a lot about the woman who seemed so wary of men. As he read further along in her journal, Jade progressed in intimacy with her lover, becoming bolder and less reserved in her explorations. The first fantasy had been sweet, an awakening of her sensuality. A testing of boundaries and establishing them. Now, she was using that sexual confidence to fulfill her secret desires. He'd found all kinds of fantasies, some playful, some intense, and a few that were downright erotic and wild, yet in none of them had she and her fantasy lover made love.

Jade's imagined lover had more willpower than he possessed, Kyle thought wryly, but then that was the crux of Jade's fantasies. She had complete control over what happened between her and her lover. And for some reason, she was avoiding the ultimate act of intimacy with the man she'd created for her private pleasure.

The way she'd physically responded to him during their midnight swim, then suddenly retreated, led Kyle to believe Jade's resistance was more of an emotional issue. Her fantasies had all the earmarkings of a passionate woman who wanted to be cherished and desired, but feared losing a vital part of herself in the richest culmination of intimacy.

He wondered what idiot had burned her badly enough to make her suspicious of the male population on such a personal, private level.

He intended to find out.

And he intended to have her.

But first, she had to be willing, her mind and emotions in sync with the demands of her body. He wanted more than superficial sex, and no less than her complete surrender.

Body and soul.

JADE GLANCED AT HER WATCH as she made her way toward the entrance of The Black Sheep, and cringed. She was forty minutes late for her five-o'clock appointment with Kyle. Her earlier appointment ran behind, then she'd gotten stuck in rush-hour traffic on Pacific Coast Highway. She'd called from her mobile phone and left a message with Kyle's bartender, Bruce, to let his boss know she was on her way.

It had been a hectic day, and although she was exhausted, she was looking forward to starting her newest project—transforming The Black Sheep into a restaurant and bar that would give Roxy's a run for their money. It was exhilarating to think that the new Black Sheep's success depended significantly on her ability to make over the place so that it would draw people into the establishment. Good food, service and atmosphere would keep them coming back.

She pushed open a heavy oak door and stepped inside. The lighting was dim, and it took her eyes a moment to adjust, though she could tell by the din of voices and raucous laughter that happy hour was well underway. A chalkboard just inside the entrance boasted tonight's drink special: Peach daiquiris.

Moving deeper into the large, sectioned building, she glanced around, taking in the raw basics she had to work with, and hoping to find Kyle in the process. The place was just as she'd imagined—a hole-in-the-wall kind of establishment. A place where people met for a casual drink after a long day at work to unwind and shoot the bull.

A scarred mahogany-and-brass bar stretched the length of one side of the room, where a good-looking, dark-haired man poured drinks and set them on the counter for the bar waitresses to deliver. Booths upholstered in red vinyl rimmed the lounge area, along with wooden tables and chairs, most of which were already taken. Sawdust covered the hardwood floor, and a game room adjoined the bar area, where customers tried their hand at darts or played pool at one of the two tables there. Musical entertainment came in the form of a jukebox belting out country-western tunes.

There was a certain appeal to the place, a warmth and friendliness that drew a person, despite the establishment's outdated furnishings and rundown appearance. From a designer's standpoint, the place showed a whole lot of promise. With the adjoining restaurant opening soon, The Black Sheep had the potential to be one of the hottest nightspots off Pacific Coast Highway.

The Black Sheep's clientele was unpretentious and laid-back, she decided. There wasn't a designer suit or stuffy executive in sight. No, the dress code slanted toward denim, leather and cowboy boots.

Dressed in a royal blue, double-breasted brocade suit and three-inch heels, she felt as out of place as a sheep in a den of wolves...and the wolves were eyeing her as if they hadn't eaten in weeks.

Shrugging off her unease, and ignoring the bawdy laughter at a nearby table, she strolled through the lounge and toward the bar. The cocktail waitress gave her a curious glance as she passed with a tray full of drinks. The bartender's gaze was speculative as well, though his smile was friendly and very welcoming.

"Excuse me, do you know where I can find Kyle?" she asked, loud enough to be heard over the din. "I had an appointment with him, and I'm a little late."

"You must be Jade." At her nod, the bartender wiped his hand on a towel and extended it toward her. She shifted her attaché and purse to her left hand and shook his hand. "I'm Bruce, the guy you spoke with on the phone. I hear you're going to give The Black Sheep a new look."

She grinned, feeling completely at ease with Bruce. "I'm going to give it my best."

"Kyle went to the storeroom to get more peaches." He shook his head ruefully and cleared the empty glasses off the bar top that the waitress had left. "I thought he was crazy when he suggested peach daiquiris for this evening's special, we don't sell a lot of them on the whole, but it seems they're pretty popular tonight."

Now I know why you always smell like peaches. Ripe, juicy peaches. I can't help but wonder if you taste just as sweet. Jade's stomach dipped at the memory of Kyle murmuring those words in her ear just a few short weeks ago. She wondered if the special was for her benefit, and couldn't contain the involuntary pleasure that spread through her at the thought.

"There he is now," Bruce said, nodding his head toward the opposite end of the bar.

"Thanks." Jade started toward Kyle, trying to keep her balance steady under the crunch of sawdust beneath her heels. The sawdust, she decided, would be one of the first things to go. Especially since it covered a beautiful hardwood floor that would gleam once it was refinished and polished.

He glanced up from the colander of fresh peeled peaches he set on the service area of the bar, and smiled. "Welcome to The Black Sheep."

Returning the smile, she slid onto the last bar stool and set her belongings in front of her. "Sorry I'm late."

His eyes danced with humor. "Thanks for calling so I didn't think you stood me up. How about a peach daiquiri?" Picking up a paring knife and a peach, he began slicing the ripe fruit, filling the blender in front of him with the fat chunks. "Tonight's special is in your honor."

Propping her elbows on the mahogany surface, she laced her fingers and rested her chin on top. "You're mighty presumptuous. What makes you think I like the *taste* of peaches?"

"Don't you?" With his brow arched mockingly, he picked up a thick, succulent wedge of peach, braced his arms on the top of the bar, and leaned toward her, teasing her bottom lip with the cool, sweet piece of fruit. Her tongue automatically darted out, catching a drop of juice before it trickled down her chin.

"Take a bite," he murmured.

It wasn't a request, but a challenge, issued in his usual bold manner. All she had to do was sit back to break the spell, but the dare in his eyes kept her from retreating. There was something about Kyle that made her feel wild, spontaneous and reckless. The lush scent of peach filled her senses, awakening a memory—a long-ago fantasy that blended the warmth of summer with slow hands sliding on her body—but then it quickly faded.

At the far end of the bar out of sight from the customers,

Jade gave in to the temptation in Kyle's eyes. She bit into the wedge of peach, and nearly groaned at the delectable sweetness that filled her mouth. Savoring the taste, she let Kyle feed her the last of the fruit until it was gone. He watched her, his eyes darkening to an arousing shade of midnight blue.

Dragging his thumb across her damp bottom lip, he brought that same finger to his mouth and sucked off the juice. "Ummm. I guess I was right after all. You do like the taste of peaches."

A pleasant hum of awareness rippled through her blood, and she managed a smile. "Yeah, I do," she admitted.

"Then you'll love my special peach daiquiri." Straightening, he grabbed another peach and finished filling the blender with the fruit.

Drawing a deep breath, Jade glanced around while Kyle prepared her drink. Bruce and the bar waitresses wore what was obviously the bar's uniform, a black T-shirt with The Black Sheep emblazoned across the chest in white lettering and black jeans. That would have to be modified, too. Nothing drastic, and the look could still be casual, but it didn't make sense to give The Black Sheep a new look without including the staff's attire as well.

Hooking the heel of one of her shoes on the brass rung at the base of her stool, she crossed one leg over the other and returned her attention to Kyle. He seemed completely at ease behind the bar, lightly flirting with the cocktail waitresses as they waited for their orders and greeting customers by name as they passed through the lounge. He excused himself from her side of the bar for a few minutes to help Bruce with the overflow of drink orders, then spoke with each patron sitting at the bar as if they were old friends before returning to finish blending her daiquiri. The atmosphere suited Kyle, and she found herself enjoying him and the friendly, laid-back ambiance of the country-western bar.

"How long have you been bartending?" she asked.

"Since I was twenty-two." He added a shot of liquor to the peach mixture in the blender and glanced up at her as he hit a button that whipped the concoction into a thick, smooth drink. "I was fresh out of the service and looking for a job. I started out as a busboy at a seafood restaurant in Venice Beach, figuring it was income until something better came along. Within six months they moved me up to bartending, and I loved it, especially meeting new people. Not an impressive career goal, but it paid the bills and kept a roof over my head."

"Oh, I don't know," she said, waving her hand to indicate everything around him, "you look pretty successful to me. It's not easy owning your own business."

A crooked smile canted his mouth, but there were shadows in his gaze that reflected a bitterness she didn't understand. And a glimpse of loneliness that made her heart catch. "It's been a long, hard road getting to this point, but it sure beats the hell out of being a lawyer."

She grinned, trying to vision Kyle in a suit and tie and a *GQ* haircut, and failed. He was too much of a rebel. "It's hard to imagine you as a stuffy lawyer."

"Too bad my father doesn't understand that." He reached for a glass and set it on the cocktail napkin he placed in front of her, then turned off the blender. "My family doesn't exactly approve of my chosen profession." After pouring the thick mixture into her glass, he poked in a straw and set a peach wedge on the rim. "Actually, when it came to me, there wasn't much they approved of at all. But I have to admit that I didn't make life easy for them. According to my father, I was nothing but trouble since I was three and crawled into his Mercedes, managed to put the car into Neutral, and coasted down the driveway and crashed into our neighbor's house."

She burst out laughing, and even though he chuckled with her, she realized that deep down, there was so much more to Kyle than his carefree ways. There was a complexity to the man that included a seemingly unsupportive family and a past tangled with resentments. Not to mention a child out of wedlock.

She ached for him, and that brief connecting emotion surprised her. She didn't want to care about Kyle, didn't want to think that beneath his flirting there was a man who had flaws. A man who might be as lonely as she, but had resigned himself to being a bachelor because it was *safe*. She identified with that feeling all too well.

Dismissing the direction of her thoughts, she lifted her glass and took a healthy sip of the drink. She made a sound of pure pleasure as a rich, creamy peach-and-vanilla flavor sank into her taste buds. This was like no drink she'd ever tasted, and knew Kyle had forever spoiled her for just any ordinary peach daiquiri.

"Good?" he asked.

"Delicious. It tastes like a peach Creamsicle." She licked her bottom lip and took another drink, wondering if Kyle had secretly discovered the way to her heart. "I have to admit that it's the best I've ever had."

"Not quite the *best* you've ever had," he said, his words oozing sexual connotation. "But we can easily change that."

Knowing he was far more potent than one-hundred-proof liquor, she said, "I'll stick to the drink."

He grinned but didn't pursue his seduction. Instead, he grabbed a damp rag and wiped down the counter. "So, what do you think of the place?"

"I think you're sitting on a potential gold mine." She swirled her straw in her glass and glanced around, seeing a piece of coal that had the ability to shine like a diamond. "The bar area is a little rustic, but once we put our ideas and suggestions together and find the right blend that keeps the casual, comfortable atmosphere you want with a more polished image, you'll appeal to a broader range of people."

He looked pleased by her quick evaluation, and excited at the prospect of implementing new changes. "That's exactly what I want. Come on, I'll give you the ten-cent tour so you can see the rest of the bar and the new restaurant."

"Okay." She slid from her stool, drink in hand. When she picked up her attaché and purse, he took them from her and with her permission, he stashed them in a cupboard behind the bar. He made sure Bruce had things under control before he led the way into the adjoining restaurant, which for the time being, was separated by a doorway draped in thick plastic. He held it aside and let her pass, then followed her through.

He flipped an electrical switch, lighting up the structure, which was in its rawest, most basic form of construction. They walked through the entire restaurant, and Jade took mental notes as she slowly sipped her drink and Kyle told her what he envisioned. On a professional level, his stylish and tasteful ideas impressed her. He wanted hunter green as the primary color, and when she suggested brass as a contrast, he agreed. When she mentioned a ballpark figure on the improvements, he didn't cringe, but instead asked if the cost covered a night out with the owner.

She'd laughed and almost said yes—that's how comfortable and relaxed she was feeling after one of his specialty drinks.

Nearly an hour later, brimming with ideas for tile samples, draperies, and upholstery selections, she followed him down a corridor just off the far end of the lounge to his office, where he had an extra set of plans to give her.

Kyle shut the door behind him and turned to find Jade taking in his sparse office furnishings, an old wooden desk, a credenza, a four-drawer file cabinet and an old worn tweed couch he'd crashed on a time or two.

She turned, her finger absently caressing the stem of her glass, empty except for the peach wedge still on the rim. "Are you planning on redecorating your office, too?"

"We might as well." He retrieved the tube and set it at the end of his desk, between his stapler and a framed picture of Christy. "What's another grand or two when I already owe the bank my life?"

She grinned in understanding. "Give it a good year or two and you'll see a big turnaround."

He smiled ruefully. "I'm counting on it."

Her expression was bright and dazzling. "From what I've seen and what we've discussed, you'll be counting your way right to a fat savings account."

He stared at her for a long minute, something deep within him shifting. He couldn't remember the last time someone had believed in him, supported him in a decision he'd made. To the outside world he was confident and sure of himself almost to the point of being cocky, but that was a facade he'd developed after years of being compared to an older brother who could do no wrong. There was always an ingrained sense of failure just beneath the surface, a feeling of inadequacy he constantly had to battle against. Unknowingly, Jade had offered him something no other person ever had: her unconditional faith in him.

Their gazes held, and gradually the tension in the room

changed, drawing tight with a heady sensuality. He breathed deeply, drawing in the scent of peaches clinging to her skin. Knowing those soft, kissable lips would taste just as delicious, and hungering for a sample, he started toward her, his advance slow and easy.

Awareness filled her eyes and she stepped back, her bottom coming into contact with the edge of his desk. "You know, it's getting late and I ought to be going."

He moved closer, trapping her between him and his desk. "Not yet," he murmured, unable to let her go until he touched her, kissed her, made her see how good they could be together.

Not until he fulfilled the fantasy he'd slowly cultivated all evening.

Relieving her of the death grip she had on her glass, he set it on his desk, then placed his hands on the silky brocade outlining the flare of her hips. She sucked in a sharp breath. He'd expected more of a physical resistance, if not a verbal one, but she wasn't denying her body's response to his touch.

Desire flared in her bright gaze, and a deep, shuddering breath escaped her. "Kyle..." Her voice was husky and damned sexy. As a protest, it wasn't much.

"Relax, Jade, and let it happen," he urged in a low, soothing voice.

She gave her head a short, frantic shake. "I...can't. We shouldn't."

Subtle fear threaded her voice, but having knowledge of its source from her fantasies—the fear of intimacy—he felt better equipped to handle her apprehension. He was taking a slow, easy, nonthreatening approach. Let *her* feel in control, even if he was the one leading.

"Yes, we should." Lifting her, he scooted her bottom back onto the edge of his desk until she was sitting on the flat surface. The movement caused her short skirt to bunch higher, giving him a glimpse of the lace band of her stockings and firm thighs.

He swallowed a groan. *Oh, man.* His heart hammered in his chest and his skin warmed and tightened. His arousal throbbed almost painfully. Slow and easy was going to kill him.

Knowing this moment would shape any chance he might have at a relationship with Jade, he furrowed his fingers into her soft, fragrant hair and used his thumbs to tilt her head up and force her to meet his gaze. "Kissing you is all I've thought about tonight. I want to know if you taste as good as you smell, like peaches. It's gonna happen, and if you let it, it can be real good."

To his surprise and pleasure, her lashes drifted shut and her lips parted. He felt her surrender, her desire. Gently he touched his mouth to her neck, skimmed his lips along her jaw. She issued a soft, surrendering moan and turned her head toward his. Feeling a spurt of triumph, he brushed his lips across hers, tenderly nuzzled them in a soft, fleeting kiss...then hovered there, a breath away from her lips.

He didn't have to wait long for her to seek his mouth. Whimpering in frustration, she dragged her hands up his arms, twined her fingers around his neck and pulled him the last inch to her satiny soft lips.

With a low, masculine groan, he gave her what she sought and what he craved. A deep, rapacious kiss. A greedy, giving, shockingly intimate kiss as lush and sweet as peach nectar.

Her fingers plowed through his hair, then slid toward his face until her palms pressed against his jaw. Not to push him away, but to pull him closer. She opened her mouth wider beneath his; he filled it with the thrusting heat of his tongue and coaxed her to give him the same.

Blindly he reached for the wedge of peach on her glass and found it. Touching the cool, damp piece of fruit just below her earlobe, he slid it to the base of her throat. She jerked back with a gasp, breaking their kiss to stare at him in shock.

A seductive grin tipped his mouth. "I want to taste you." Before she could do or say anything he lowered his head and followed the path of the peach with his tongue, swirling, gliding downward, lapping the sticky sweetness in long, slow provocative strokes.

His free hand worked the buttons of her jacket, and once it fell open he eased it down her arms, leaving her clad in the laciest, sexiest bra he'd ever seen. In less than a heartbeat he'd unsnapped the front closure and her breasts spilled forward, her nipples tight and hard. The erotic sight of her half-naked on his desk, her breasts growing full as he watched, and her skirt shoved high around her thighs, was enough to make him weak in the knees. He groaned deep in his throat, a low male sound that combined masculine appreciation and a deeper, more elemental need no other woman had ever evoked in him.

He glanced up. Jade's eyes were shut. He supposed that was the best way for her to experience her fantasy, but he wanted her to look at him, know exactly who was satisfying her deepest desires.

"Jade, open your eyes," he whispered. "I want you to watch the way your body responds to me."

Her lashes fluttered open, and his heart caught at the hint of vulnerability he saw in the depth of her eyes. Determined to replace her apprehension with pleasure, he glided the peach down the slope of one breast and leisurely circled her nipple until it was stiff and wet with nectar. She trembled, and he continued to the other breast, giving the tip equal attention while waiting patiently for her to grant him the liberty to appease his appetite for her, and to experience the sweet flavor of peaches on warmed skin.

A deep, internal shudder rippled through Jade at the hot, lustful look in Kyle's eyes as he painted her breasts with the fragrant wedge of fruit. Her head swam from the intoxicating scent filling her every breath, and she could feel herself growing warm and damp...and shamefully aroused. Almost as if they had a will of their own, her thighs tightened around his hips, drawing him closer....

This was wicked. Decadent. But she couldn't bring herself to stop. She thought again of the fantasy he'd tapped into, and knew she wanted to feel his mouth on her. Just this once....

Very tentatively her hands touched his shoulders and eased around his neck. Sinking her fingers into his hair, she drew his mouth to her breasts. The first touch of his tongue electrified her, and then she got lost in the thrilling, frenzied riot of sensations. His lips and tongue were at once tender and greedy with his exploration. He bathed her skin with infinite care, licked the sensitive curve of her breasts, and curled his tongue around her nipple. Then finally—oh, God, *finally*—he suckled the aching crest deep into his mouth.

She felt out of control, frightened by how fast and easy it was to lose herself with Kyle. It only took a gentle tug on his hair for him to lift his head, making her realize how in tune he was to *her*, and not the demands of his own body. The restraint she saw in his dark eyes was admirable.

He smiled, his lashes falling half-mast. "You taste just as sweet as you smell." Slipping the rest of the peach into his mouth, he brought his sticky fingers to her parted lips, then slid one long finger into her mouth. Automatically, brazenly, she swirled her tongue around the tip.

He groaned and withdrew his finger, lingering for a moment on her soft, kiss-swollen lips. "You do that well," he said huskily.

Her face flushed at his meaning. In gradual increments, cognizance returned and finally hit her like a dose of cold water. "Oh, Lord," she groaned in embarrassment, pressing her hands to her flaming cheeks. "I can't believe that you, that we...that I..." *I can't believe that a fantasy could be even better in reality.*

He chuckled, the sound strained. "Yeah, that was pretty damned incredible."

What had she done? She shook her head in dismay and fumbled with her bra, trying her best to snap the front closure while her hands shook. "This is definitely *not* a good idea." She managed to button her jacket though it hung on her in a haphazard way, and tried to wriggle around him.

He backed away, just enough so he wasn't crowded between her slim thighs, but kept her pinned to his desk by bracing his hands on the edge on either side of her. "After the way you nearly came apart for me, there's no way I'm going to let you dismiss me or what just happened with a quick, easy exit. Give me one good reason why you think we aren't a good idea and I'll consider it."

"I don't mix business and pleasure," she said primly.

His mouth lifted in a lazy smile. "If you expect me to choose between the two, it's pleasure all the way."

Jade shivered at the thought of the endless pleasure this man was capable of giving her. "Kyle, I'm not looking to get involved with anyone."

"Sweetheart," he said, his tone patient, "what we just

shared is enough to tell me you're more involved than you think."

She frowned at him for being so rude as to point out the obvious. "I don't have time in my life for emotional entanglements."

"Then how about a no-strings-attached affair?" he offered, but there was something else in his gaze that gave his words a deeper meaning and contradicted his flippant offer.

"I don't go for casual sex." Heck, she hadn't had sex, casual or otherwise, in three years!

"Neither do I," he reassured her. "There's a chemistry between us, we both feel it, so why not go with it and see where it leads?"

Because she was afraid of where it might lead, afraid of getting so lost in emotions that she forgot all the things that were important to her. Her identity, her independence, being in control...

Unexpectedly he swooped down and captured her lips in a hot, thorough, needy kiss she automatically returned with maddening fervor. Finally he lifted his mouth from hers, leaving her feeling antsy and eager and restless.

Masculine satisfaction glittered in his eyes. He tucked a stray strand of hair behind her ear, his fingers lingering there, making her go all shivery inside. "I want to be lovers, in every sense of the word," he told her.

"So, you want sex," she said flatly.

"Yes, eventually, when *you're* ready to make love," he said, putting the emphasis on her calling the shots. "An affair isn't just about sex. It's a seduction of the mind, senses and ultimately the body. We'll take things slow and easy or fast and wild. You set the pace."

She stared into his eyes, drawn like never before. For the first time in a long time she physically wanted a man, slow and easy *and* fast and wild. A no-holds-barred wanting, no caution, no restraints. A satisfaction of mutual wants, needs and desires. What he was offering her was exciting and thrilling. And she wanted this fling. With him. For as long as the attraction and fascination lasted. Without the complication of any emotional entanglements.

Especially that.

She grew giddy with anticipation. Isn't that what her independence was all about? The freedom to make her own choices, control any situation to her liking? To give only as much as she wanted and walk away when it was over, emotions intact?

Absolutely.

And for the first time in three years she wanted to test that feminine power, and Kyle was giving her the perfect opportunity.

Taking a deep breath, she plunged headlong into the forbidden before she lost the nerve. "All right," she agreed. "We'll have an affair."

5

"YOU'RE DAYDREAMING again."

Jade started at the sound of Mariah's amused voice and jerked her head in the direction of her office door, where her sister stood. Daydreaming didn't even begin to describe the scrumptious fantasy she'd been weaving in her mind. She shuffled paperwork on her desk in an attempt to look busy, but couldn't remember what she'd been doing before Kyle had invaded her thoughts and she'd drifted off to a forbidden dimension. Damn, she had to get a grip before she became completely obsessed with Kyle and the affair she'd agreed to. Or maybe it was the anticipation of their tryst that had her so preoccupied.

"I was, uh, just, um...thinking." Good Lord, when had she become such a scatterbrain that she couldn't even talk without tripping all over her tongue?

Dressed in an emerald green jumpsuit with a gold braided belt, Mariah sauntered into Jade's office, a piece of paper crinkling in her hand. "You seem to be doing a lot of that lately. Thinking, that is," she clarified, a Cheshire-cat grin curling the corners of her mouth. "Would Kyle Stephens be the reason?"

Was she that transparent? Jade's face warmed and she shifted in her high-back tweed chair. "What makes you say that?"

"This." Standing across from her, Mariah released the

paper in her hand, and the document fluttered to Jade's messy desktop.

Stalling the inevitable, Jade gave the familiar name and business typed on the contract a nonchalant glance. "Oh, that."

"Yes, *that*." Exasperation tinged Mariah's voice. "Why didn't you tell me you'd acquired Kyle Stephens as a client?"

She shrugged. "I knew you'd see a copy of the contract." As partners, they each received a copy of all contracts, no matter who acquired them, so they both knew their client base should either of them need to take over an account.

"You could have told me personally," Mariah said, crossing her arms over her chest.

Jade flashed a sugary sweet smile. "Why, so you could interrogate me?"

Mariah pursed her lips at Jade's direct hit. "How can I not? Last I remember you didn't want to have anything to do with Kyle Stephens. Then a few weeks later I find a contract for you to refurbish his bar and decorate his restaurant, which is quite an impressive account for Casual Elegance. You can't blame me for being a little curious."

"It's just another business deal, Riah." And so was their affair—a transaction based on their mutual attraction and desire. Once the passion and thrill fizzled, they'd go their separate ways, which she estimated should be right around the time she finished decorating his bar and restaurant.

"Sure it is," Mariah murmured, her shrewd look not buying into the simple premise. She settled into the chair in front of Jade's desk, and just as Jade dreaded, the cross-examination began. "The Black Sheep might be a business deal, but I want to know what's going on between you and Kyle on a personal level. Hopefully more than business."

Jade leaned back in her chair and considered her sister's comment. She didn't think Mariah would understand her decision to have a capricious affair with Kyle, not after what her sister had been through with Grey. Mariah believed solidly in commitment, love and the sanctity of marriage. There was no in-between with Mariah, and she'd never settle for an impetuous fling for the sake of mutual pleasure. Luckily Mariah had swayed Grey to her way of thinking.

An unexpected pang of sadness ribboned through her. Once, a long time ago, she'd had faith in a committed relationship, too. But her own lesson in what she'd thought was love had made her cynical.

Damn you, Adam Beckman, she thought, hating that his past influence could still affect certain aspects of her life in the present. Like her trust in men and their motives.

As much as she tried denying not wanting or needing a man in her life, that lonely, empty part of her still yearned to find someone special. Someone steady, strong, yet gentle and giving when it counted. Someone who'd give her the freedom to do what she wanted, and didn't demand more than she was able to give. Someone who'd accept her for the real woman she was beneath the flamboyance and sass.

Someone like Kyle.

Startled by that thought, she dismissed it as meaningless and frivolous, considering he'd admitted to being a confirmed bachelor. And even though he'd promised her she'd be in control of how fast and far their affair went, she knew and accepted up-front that theirs wasn't a forever kind of relationship. That knowledge should have brought her relief, but left her with an elusive feeling of wanting.

"Well?" Mariah prompted.

Jade blinked at her sister, thinking back to the question that had put her on a tangent better left unexplored. Oh, yeah, she wanted to know what was going on between her and Kyle on a personal level.

"We're just..." The right word eluded Jade. What were they? They weren't lovers, at least not yet. And they'd never be a "couple." And their association encompassed more than a business relationship.

Mariah drummed her fingernails on the wooden arm-rest of her chair. "You're just *what?*"

Pushy broad. "We're just friends," she answered indifferently. Certainly she and Kyle were at least that.

"Oh." The tiny frown of disappointment creasing Mariah's brows gave way to a slow, mischievous smile. Standing, she grabbed her copy of the contract off Jade's desk and winked at her. "Well, you never know where friendship can lead."

Jade shook her head at her sister's optimism. Mariah just smiled and turned to go, but stopped when their receptionist's voice drifted out of Jade's intercom.

"Jade, there's a Kyle Stephens here to see you. He doesn't have an appointment, but he's insisting you'll see him without one," Pam said, her exasperation plain. "What would you like me to do?"

Kyle Stephens, bold as he pleased. Jade's pulse picked up at the mere thought, warming her insides with every heartbeat. "Send him to my office," she said to Pam, then disconnected the line with a push of a button on the phone.

"He certainly doesn't lack in the confidence department, does he?" Mariah commented, her tone filled with amusement.

If Mariah knew the half of how brazen and self-assured Kyle was, she'd be shocked. "He's a client, which gives him certain privileges, like dropping by without an appointment." Her handy excuse sounded good, though she had to admit she was curious about why he hadn't mentioned anything about stopping by when she'd left The Black Sheep last night. But then again, after his seduction and her surrender, her mind had been on anything but business.

Jade waited for Mariah to continue out her office, and when she realized her sister needed a little prompting, she stood and waved a hand toward the entrance. "The door is right behind you, just in case you forgot the way *out*."

Expression aghast, Mariah affected a prim and proper look that would have made Miss Manners proud. "I wouldn't dream of being so rude as to not say hello."

Glaring, Jade opened her mouth to issue a retort, but the remark died on her lips at the sound of a brisk knock. Her gaze shifted over her sister's shoulder to the sinfully sexy man standing in the doorway. Then nothing seemed to matter as she connected with dark blue eyes, soft and rich as velvet, and as warm as sunshine caressing her bare skin. A honeyed heat of awareness sluiced through her veins, settling in feminine places gone too long without a man's touch. It was Kyle whom she wanted to ease the ache. Kyle, with a mouth that delivered hot, exciting kisses and strong hands that promised a wealth of pleasure.

Grinning that lazy, bad-boy grin of his, he strolled into her office, filling the room with his masculine presence. He wore a pair of Levi's, faded in all the right places, and a blue chambray shirt, the sleeves rolled to midforearm. "Good afternoon, ladies."

"Kyle," Mariah said, reaching out to clasp his hand in greeting. "It's so nice to see you again. Jade was just telling me you're a new client of ours."

"Yes, I am," he said, his tone warm and pleasant. "I'm looking forward to working with Jade."

"Umm," Mariah murmured thoughtfully, a mischievous smile curving her mouth. "Well, I'll let the two of you discuss whatever it is you need to discuss." She turned to leave, but stopped in the doorway, one hand resting on the frame as she glanced back at Jade. "Oh, I almost forgot!"

Jade slowly rounded her desk, not trusting her sister's wide-eyed innocence. "Forgot what?"

Mariah smiled sweetly—too sweetly for Jade's liking. "I talked to Mom this morning and she mentioned having a family barbecue at their place for your birthday next weekend. I'm sure they wouldn't mind if you brought Kyle along, him being a *friend* and all."

Jade forced a smile, though her fingers itched to strangle her meddling sister. "I don't think Kyle would be interested—"

"I'd love to go," he interrupted, bestowing a dazzling, charming smile on Mariah that any woman would be hard-pressed to resist. "Thanks for the invitation."

Mariah grinned. "My pleasure." Before Jade could object, Mariah ducked safely from the room and closed the door behind her.

Damn her sister, anyway, Jade thought irritably. Her relationship with Kyle wasn't supposed to get cozy, and meeting her parents was too cozy for comfort. She preferred to keep their affair private—the less her family knew about Kyle, the better, because this wasn't going to be a lasting relationship.

She glanced up at Kyle, who stood next to her. His gaze,

she couldn't help noticing, was focused on her mouth, which made it difficult for her to concentrate. "My sister can be a bit pushy at times," she said, attempting to change his mind about joining her family get-together. "You really don't have to go."

The corner of his mouth crooked in a half smile. "I really want to."

Did she really expect Kyle to concede so easily? She drew a deep breath and opted for honesty. "The truth is...I haven't brought a male friend home in a long time." Not since Adam, and the significance of bringing Kyle to meet her parents wasn't something she was ready for.

"I'll be a perfect gentleman," he promised.

He didn't understand the complications of openly acknowledging their *relationship*. "I don't want my parents to get the wrong idea about us, or get their hopes up for something more between us than there is."

He slid his hands into the front pockets of his well-worn jeans. "Which is?"

"Well, an affair." Feeling exasperated and flustered beneath his intense stare, she went back to her desk and shuffled papers. "My father will drive you nuts with the third degree about our relationship and your intentions—"

"Trust me, tiger," he said in a soothing drawl. "I can handle your father and any questions he might have. And I'd never do or say anything to embarrass you."

She met his gaze from across the desk. "I never said you would." The thing was, he was so unpredictable, and having an affair was so foreign to her, she didn't know what to expect from him, or their newly established relationship. Or what *he* expected from *her*. The whole idea of being intimate with Kyle was at once scary and thrilling.

"I'll tell you what—if you still feel this way by next

weekend, I'll respect your wishes and not go to your parents'. The decision will be yours."

"Okay." She hadn't realized how tense the whole subject made her until she felt her body relax. He was giving her the space she needed, and she was grateful for that.

His gaze turned warm and speculative. "So, how old are you going to be, anyway?"

Her mouth pursed in displeasure. She was having a difficult enough time dealing with the fact that she was hitting a major milestone in her life without voicing it aloud. "Don't ask," she muttered.

His rich, amused chuckles filled her office. "It can't be that bad. Come on, 'fess up."

She sighed, knowing she had to get used to the idea of getting older, but she didn't have to like it. "I'm going to be the big 3-0." She cringed as she said the number.

"Oh, yeah, that puts you way over the hill," he teased. "I'll be sure to get you a cane and a bottle of Geritol."

She made a face at him, though deep down inside she couldn't stop thinking that she'd once imagined having a husband and family by now—but the future looked mighty bleak on that score. When she saw Mariah with Grey and Kayla, and how happy they were as a family, she sometimes experienced a twinge of envy that made her wonder if she was destined to live her life alone. It was a possibility, considering her timidity toward committing herself to another man.

Not caring for the direction of those thoughts, she reached for The Black Sheep's file, which she'd left in her "pending" basket on the corner of her desk. "So, what brings you by? We didn't have an appointment to sign your contract until tomorrow morning."

"My visit has nothing to do with my contract." Eyes glittering with purpose, he strolled toward where she stood behind her desk. "You see, I've got this problem, and it's all your fault. And since it's your fault, I think you ought to do something about it."

He stopped behind her, but didn't touch her. All at once she was aware of the silence and intimacy of her office. That they were totally and completely alone, and she still didn't know why he was there. Could only imagine the reason for his visit.

A shiver of anticipation danced down her spine and settled in the pit of her belly. The Black Sheep's file slipped from her fingers and landed on the paperwork on her blotter.

"What's all my fault?" she asked breathlessly.

"That I can't stop thinking about you. About the way you smell..." Lowering his head, he drew a deep breath of her scent. "The way you feel..." Slowly he dragged his hands over the curve of her hips. "And the way you taste. Especially that. You taste like sweet peaches and rich cream...."

A moan caught in her throat. Resisting the urge to lean back against him and absorb his heat, she struggled to maintain her composure. Business was always a good diffuser.

She turned around, breaking the contact of his hands, but trapping herself in a more precarious situation—between him and her desk. "Uh, since you're here you might as well sign your contract now."

"In a minute," he murmured, his long, tawny lashes sweeping downward.

Sifting his fingers through the wispy hair at the side of her face, he lifted her mouth to his. Her lips automatically parted, and she accepted the blatantly erotic, very thorough French kiss he gave her. A purring rumble rose up in her throat, and he returned the sound of pleasure with a masculine growl of his own.

A part of her mind not overwhelmed by desire wondered how far he planned to take their kiss...if he'd come to her office to seduce her and make their affair official. He moved closer, pressing his body against hers. His erection strained against her belly, and a frisson of panic doused the flames that had burned so brightly only moments before.

As much as she wanted Kyle, as much as she enjoyed his kisses and caresses, she still felt unsure of him, herself and *them* to advance to the next level of intimacy.

As if he sensed her emotional withdrawal, he ended the kiss and took a small step back.

"Damn," he said softly, a lopsided grin full of masculine satisfaction on his face. "If I'd known how incredibly sexy and soft your mouth felt, no way would I have waited six months to kiss you."

She willed her heart rate to stabilize, and reached for some much needed sass. "I'm surprised you waited at all, considering how presumptuous you are."

His dark blue eyes sparkled with humor. "It's always nice to have the other person's cooperation when you try and kiss her. I didn't want to find out if you had a strong left hook." He touched her cheek, ran a fingertip along her jaw. "Now, about my contract?"

Collecting her poise, and welcoming the business diversion, she turned toward her desk, retrieved his contract from his file, and handed it to him. "These are just approximate figures and are estimated on the high side until we get the proposal for your restaurant and bar completely laid out, which we'll start on next week. Read through the preliminary contract, and if everything meets with your approval sign on the dotted line."

Mr. Presumptuous settled himself into her high-back chair and propped his boots on the corner of her desk, confining her to a cramped triangle constructed of his legs, her chair and her desk. He began perusing the contract, seemingly oblivious to the fact that she was trapped, and that he was sitting in *her* seat.

No way was she going to take one of the chairs in front of her desk reserved for clients and let him be in the dominant position, so she eased back onto the flat surface of her desk, crossed one leg over the other, and waited for him to finish reading the terms of their agreement.

After a few silent moments passed, he glanced up at her. "Got a pen?"

Remembering what had transpired the last time he'd made such a request, she held the pen just out of his reach. "Depends on where you plan to put your signature."

He chuckled and ran a finger along the hem of her skirt, then lifted the edge half an inch as if to peek underneath. "You got a dotted line somewhere I don't know about?"

Her thigh tingled where he touched, and she swatted his hand away before he got any bolder. "No," she answered.

"Then you're safe," he said, plucking the pen from her grasp. "For now."

She watched him sign his name in a bold, indecipherable scrawl. "Casual Elegance needs half of the estimated amount as a deposit, and we'll bill you for the balance at the completion of the project. You can mail the deposit or I can stop by the bar and pick it up—"

"I've got a check on me." He shifted in the chair, pulled his wallet from his back pocket, then withdrew a folded check. "I always keep a spare on me for emergencies."

Less than a minute later she held a fair chunk of change in her hand. The check, written on a business account un-

der the name The Black Sheep, had a single black sheep
graphic in the upper left-hand corner. She'd decided she
liked the catchy and original name.

Paper-clipping the check to his file for Pam to process,
she glanced up at him, and asked curiously, "So, how did
you come up with the name The Black Sheep?"

Kyle leaned back in Jade's chair and briefly contemplated her question, and the complicated and personal answer he'd never expected to have to explain to anyone.
"It's a long story," he said dismissively. "As long as I am
old."

His comment didn't dissuade her. If anything, the interest in her gaze intensified. "Then how about giving me
the condensed version?"

She didn't take a hint very well, he thought, slightly disgruntled. He could have ended their discussion with a
vague, "Inspiration struck." His past wasn't something
he was proud of, but how could he expect her to open up
with him if he refused to do the same?

Knowing how important this moment of trust and sharing was to their relationship, he met her gaze. "I named
the bar The Black Sheep because it's who and what I am,"
he said, simplifying his reasons the best he could. "The
black sheep of the Stephens' family. The rebellious son
who was always a disappointment."

A small smile touched her lips, still a little swollen from
his kiss. "All kids are rebellious at one point or another in
their teenage years. It's a stage we all go through."

It had been more than a developmental stage, he
thought. It had been a lifetime of not being able to live up
to his father's expectations and of being constantly compared to his older brother. No matter how hard he'd tried
to please his father, he'd *never* been as good as Nathan.

And Nathan had been far from a saint, just the firstborn

son who'd learned early how to manipulate their father, and cover his ass when things went wrong by blaming Kyle.

"My rebellion started when I was seven and my mother died," he said, remembering how his mother had tried to buffer his father's favoritism when she'd been alive. After her death, there'd been no one to defuse the friction among him, his brother and his father. His new step-mother hadn't had much patience for the bundle of energy he'd been and found it easier to ignore him than deal with the problem. "And it didn't end until I was eighteen and my father finally disowned me."

Her eyes widened in astonishment and shock. "What did you do that would make your father so mad he'd disown you?"

The tension tightening Kyle's shoulders made him all too aware that the resentment and anger he'd experienced as a youth was deep and buried, but certainly not forgotten. "I was a regular juvenile delinquent," he admitted, though his defiance had been a deliberate attempt to defy his father. "The only thing that kept me out of jail, and the Stephens' name out of a nasty scandal, was my father's money and his influence as a lawyer. But they got a scandal anyway the summer I got Jamie Ann pregnant, chose not to marry her, then joined the marines, which wasn't exactly what my father had planned for my future."

"So, you don't talk to your family?" She asked the question tentatively, as if she couldn't quite believe it was true.

"I haven't in years. My brother is a self-absorbed, cut-throat lawyer who has made my father proud. I have a little stepsister, Veronica, who is the only one who stays in touch." Ironically, she was the only real connection he had to a family who'd basically written him off. "When she told my brother and father I'd opened up a bar, my fa-

ther said I'd sunk to new lows. How's that for being supportive?"

She shook her head in dismay. "I can't imagine what it
would be like not to have a close family. My parents have
always been so wonderfully supportive, and my sister is
like my best friend. We share everything. Well, just about
everything," she clarified, remembering what she'd chosen not to tell her sister.

"You're lucky. I've never really been a part of my family. I've always been the outsider looking in." Like a kid
with his nose pressed to a candy-store window, wanting
the goodies, but never allowed to step inside to buy them.
"I'm happy here in California, and even though it's been
a struggle at times being on my own, I've earned everything I have without the influence of the Stephens' name
or money."

But it had taken him a long time to get to that point in
his life, to come to terms with his past and the mistakes
and choices he'd made. Choices that included forfeiting
watching his daughter grow into the young woman she
was today.

There had been times when he'd wished he could be a
part of a family who accepted him for who and what he
was, but long ago realized he was better off on his own.
No expectations, except the ones he set for himself. No
ties or commitments, which meant he had no one to disappoint or fail.

The phone on Jade's desk buzzed, and she started at the
interruption, then excused herself to reach for the receiver
and take the call.

Kyle scrubbed a hand along his jaw and sank back into
the chair, watching as she talked to a client. Jade was sexy,
sweet and vulnerable in a way she'd never admit to, but
strong in all the ways that mattered. Those facets drew

him, seduced him, as did her fantasies that revealed so much about the woman she was. The woman he intended to claim and brand as his own, which was a startling revelation considering he'd never been the barbaric, possessive type.

She hung up the phone and gave him an apologetic look. "I'm sorry about that."

"Don't be. Business comes first." And he'd never interfere with something so obviously important to her. He stood. "I've got to get going anyway. I'm meeting with the electrician at the restaurant in about half an hour."

She nodded and slid from her desk, so that they stood a foot apart. Thrusting his hands into the front pockets of his jeans to keep from pulling her closer, he dipped his head toward her. She automatically lifted her lips, and he bypassed that particular temptation and gave her a quick, chaste goodbye kiss on her cheek.

He drew back, noting the confusion in her eyes, and a little disappointment, too. He smothered a grin. His little tiger had expected something wilder, sexier. "I'll talk to you later?"

"Sure." Her brows creased, enhancing her uncertain expression. "Kyle, about our...affair."

He tilted his head and smiled. "Yes?"

"When you came here today..." She shook her head, and absently chewed on her bottom lip, as if trying to gather her thoughts. "I'm not sure I know what to expect from our...relationship."

Certainly not his life history, he thought, inwardly grimacing. And then her hesitancy dawned on him. "Did you think I came here today to demand my first sexual favor?"

"Well, I have to admit that I wasn't sure." She laughed, but the sound was filled with a wealth of insecurities. "It's not like I've had a whole lot of experience at this kind of thing."

Something warm and unexplainable touched his heart at that moment. "I stopped by today because I wanted to see you, not for any other ulterior motive." He gave in to the urge and brushed his fingers along her cheek, then dragged his thumb along her jaw. "To be honest, I don't think we're ready to make love." But that didn't mean they couldn't enjoy a little mental and physical foreplay, or act out a fantasy or two of hers. "I want to get to know *you*, Jade. I'm hoping we can become good friends as well as lovers."

Jade pulled in a deep breath while considering Kyle's words, wondering if she was capable of giving him everything he expected from her, without losing that vital part of herself she'd spent three years conditioning.

"You've got that look in your eyes," he murmured. "Why?"

Her gaze jerked to his. "What look?"

"Panic. Fear."

She didn't like being that transparent. Didn't like that he was so connected to her feelings and emotions. It was startling and disarming and made her put her guard up.

"What are you afraid of?" he asked softly. "Do you think I'll hurt you?"

She swallowed hard. How could he know her so well, without really knowing her at all? Physically, she knew he'd never harm her. Emotionally, she feared he'd destroy her if she let him.

It was all a matter of staying in charge of her emotional self. No problem.

Or was it?

"Of course not," she said breezily, ending the whole subject by turning around and shuffling through the files and papers on her desk. "I've got tons of work to get through—"

"Say no more, I'm outta here." He started for the door, but stopped short of opening it. He glanced over his shoulder, his gaze kind. "Just so you know, I'd never deliberately hurt you. You've got to let yourself trust me, Jade."

With that, he walked out of her office, leaving her to wonder if it was him she didn't trust or herself.

KYLE STEPPED BENEATH the hot shower spray in an attempt to unwind and relax after a long day and night at The Black Sheep. Friday nights at the bar were usually busy, but tonight's crowd surpassed any other weekend record, in attendance and profits. From what he'd gleaned from the new customers he'd had a chance to chat with, word was already spreading about the new restaurant and plans to refurbish the bar.

As a result of the unexpected boom in business, he'd had to give up a promising evening with Jade in order to assist Bruce with the overflow of drink orders. He'd planned on taking her on their first real date: dinner at a nice, intimate restaurant overlooking the ocean where they could talk, then afterward a leisurely, romantic stroll along the beach.

Business had intruded on that great idea.

When he'd called her to apologize for canceling, she'd understood his reasons, much to his relief. The past couple of days since he'd dropped by her office unannounced they'd established a comfortable, easy friendship. She'd finally given him her phone number so he could call, and just this morning he'd stopped by her condo, surprising her with fresh-baked muffins and Irish cream coffee for breakfast. They'd spent an hour talking and laughing, los-

ing track of time until she'd absently glanced up at the
kitchen clock and realized if she didn't leave for the office,
she was going to be late for an appointment.

He didn't so much as kiss her, knowing how difficult it
was to stop at one taste, one touch. Nearly impossible,
though it had been just as hard not to take advantage of
their "affair" and steal a kiss or two...or three.

He'd been pleasantly surprised when she'd shown up
at The Black Sheep a few hours after he'd canceled their
date, to sit at the bar and have a drink while he tended
bar. She hadn't demanded his time, just accepted whatever attention and quick conversation he could give her in
between the tasks of filling drink orders, waiting on tables
to help the cocktail waitresses and clearing off the bar as
customers came and went.

While mixing martinis, blending frozen drinks and refilling bowls of pretzels and peanuts, he'd decided if he
wanted to spend more time with Jade, he needed to hire
another bartender, if not two when the restaurant opened.
Business was flourishing, and fast, and he could no longer
operate with a small crew and give the patrons the quick,
friendly service he wanted associated with The Black
Sheep. He wasn't one of those owners willing to sacrifice
good service for a small payroll.

Bracing his hands on the tiled shower wall, he dipped
his head beneath the pounding spray, letting the hot water drench his hair and sluice over his shoulders and
down his back. Then he reached for the soap and lathered
up.

As a first date with Jade, the evening had been unexpectedly enjoyable, although frustrating because of his inability to completely focus only on her as he'd wanted to.
But she hadn't seemed to mind. While he worked, she
sipped the peach daiquiri he'd made her and plugged

quarters into the jukebox even though she'd claimed not to like country-western music. When he'd teased her about her frequent trips, she'd sheepishly admitted that certain songs were starting to grow on her.

He was more than a little relieved when she turned down at least half a dozen requests to dance—if anyone was going to teach her to two-step, it would be himself. His territorial thoughts might not have stopped a few of the regulars from ogling her and the tight jeans and form-fitting, low-cut T-shirt she wore, but the off-limits look he cast their way made his message loud and clear.

She was his.

Jade had sat at what he was beginning to think of as "her spot" at the far end of the bar, watching the games of pool and darts in the adjoining room while jotting decorating ideas on a legal pad. She'd shared her notes and a soft smile with him when there had been a lull, which hadn't been often enough. The time he'd given her had been brief, flirting, and over too soon before the next wave of drink orders swamped him and Bruce.

The women he'd dated since acquiring The Black Sheep didn't understand his any-time-of-the-day-or-night commitment to his business. Most had been under the misconception that since he owned the place, he had nothing but free time on his hands. None realized it was his dedication to the establishment, employees and patrons that made the place flourish and prosper to the point that he could justify adding the restaurant. Jade understood the unanticipated burdens and responsibilities a business required, and accepted the sometimes intrusive duties an owner was obliged to manage. She made no demands on him to choose between her and his business, gave no guilt trips for last-minute cancellations and more important obligations. Instead, she'd made the best of the situation.

And when she couldn't conceal her tired yawns any longer, he'd sent her home, promising her they were still on for the following morning to meet at The Black Sheep to start on her decorating consultation.

Her support meant a lot to him, he realized as he stepped from the shower and grabbed a towel. His own family didn't condone his chosen career, or anything else he'd ever done in his life. And although he'd grown to not give a damn what his family thought of him, it was suddenly important that Jade knew him for the responsible, reliable man he'd become.

What about keeping her journal a secret? his conscience taunted. The journal, he justified, had been up for sale and anybody could have bought it. He'd just been at the right place at the right time. No way could he regret reading Jade's fantasies, or fulfilling them, not when those intimate fantasies were the only chance he had of getting close enough to break past Jade's defenses.

Yet there was still so much he didn't know about her. So much he'd yet to discover and understand.

Shoving his fingers through his damp hair, he strolled into his bedroom and pulled on a pair of cotton shorts. It was past two in the morning, but he wasn't tired, and the burgundy bound treasure tucked in his nightstand beckoned. The lure of Jade's sensual, sexy stories was always stronger than he could resist, and he gave into the temptation to indulge. Pushing his pillows against the headboard of his bed, he settled himself on the mattress, opened the journal to the last page he'd marked and began to read the entry.

The garden was dark and full of shadows, but she had nothing to fear. She was with her lover and felt safe and protected. Hand clasped in his, she followed him deeper into the night, knowing he intended to seduce her...and wanting him to. The heady fragrance drifting from the rosebushes lining the cobblestone walkway filled her every breath, the scent as arousing as the anticipation of her lover's touch.

When they reached the high stone wall enclosing the garden, she waited for him to come to her, to embrace her, to kiss and touch her.

A slow, sensual smile curved his mouth. "Put your hands on the wall and keep them there."

Heart pounding wildly, she laid her palms against the smooth, cool stones. For a moment, the position made her feel vulnerable, then the warmth and strength of his body pressed along her back, comforting and familiar. He murmured soothing reassurances into her ear as his fingers attempted to unbutton her gauze blouse. She grew anxious and excited.

Urgency made her thrust her unbound breasts toward his hands. A whimper of frustration rolled from her throat, and he answered the needy sound by impatiently ripping open her blouse. He filled his palms with her breasts, kneading the aching flesh before his hands skimmed down her belly, over her gauze skirt, then beneath the hem.

He touched the inside of her thighs, coaxed them apart with the pressure of his hands. She complied, eager and restless for what she knew he could give her. For what she wanted. His breath was hot and heavy on her neck, his body hard and demanding behind hers.

His fingers slipped under the elastic band of her panties, stroking her, then slipping deeper...until she lost herself in an exquisite climax that seemed to have no ending, only ripples of sensation and pleasure that went on forever....

6

"WHAT DO YOU THINK of this Naugahyde for the booths? It's the same dark shade of green as the window treatments you selected, and it even has flecks of gold in the material. It's a perfect match, don't you think?"

On some distant plane, Kyle heard Jade's words, but sometime in the past half hour his mind had drifted back to last night's fantasy, mulling over how he could make that erotic journal entry of Jade's a reality. It's not as though he had a rose garden at his disposal. But he was a creative kind of guy—it was just a matter of finding the right opportunity and using it to his advantage. And he was confident the perfect moment *would* present itself, just like the other times had.

He looked across the table at Jade as she chattered on about the benefits of Naugahyde. They were sitting in a corner booth in The Black Sheep, surrounded by fabric swatches, books of window treatment designs and catalogs of decorative accessories for the bar and restaurant. She really knew her business and had an exceptional eye for design. For the most part, he'd gone with her recommendations.

Since it was Saturday, and warm at that, she was dressed casually in a silky peach-colored camisole that buttoned down the front, and a short denim skirt. Her legs were tanned and bare, and she'd worn flat sandals with peach and gold straps. She looked as fresh and natural as the sweet peach scent clinging to her skin. Even her eyes, today a warm gold hue, complemented her outfit.

"We can use it to reupholster the booths and the bar stools in the lounge," she was saying of the Naugahyde, even as she jotted the order on an invoice. "Maybe go with a tuck and roll or diamond tuft design. And then we can use the hunter green and gold tweed in the restaurant to tie the two together. With the window valances and brass trim, the place will look fabulous." She looked up, her eyes bright and expectant. "What do you think?"

She'd be shocked if she knew what he was thinking...imagining her soft breasts in his hands, the warmth of her thighs beneath his fingertips, the catch of her breath as he caressed her in soft, sensitive places....

"Kyle?" she said, her tone exasperated.

He blinked, focusing on her face and the tiny frown creasing her brow. "Uh, yeah, fine," he said, giving himself a firm mental shake out of Jade's fantasy and into the present.

"You're not even paying attention." She tucked a wispy cinnamon strand of hair behind her ear, and the thin gold bracelets on her wrists jangled. "Are you okay? You seem like you're not quite here. Did I lose you somewhere along the way?"

He sat up straighter and gave her an apologetic look. "Sorry, I kind of drifted there for a couple of minutes." An understatement, but as good excuse as any. "It was a late night and I'm still feeling the effects." At least that was pure truth.

She reached across the table and patted his hand, feigning a sympathetic expression. "Poor baby."

"More than you know," he muttered.

A delicate brow arched. "Excuse me?"

He shook his head, not willing to explain his cryptic comment. "Nothing. Now, what were you saying?"

A charitable, understanding smile touched her lips. "That maybe we need a break." She closed her invoice booklet and capped her pen. "We've been at this for three hours, and we've actually accomplished most of what I need to get started. The little things we'll decide on as needed."

"Then how about lunch?" he offered, not quite ready to let her leave. They hadn't had much time for anything but business since he'd visited her at her office. This opportunity was too prime to waste. "I can hardly let you leave without feeding you first. There's a deli nearby that delivers."

Her stomach growled as if on cue, and they both laughed. "I guess I am a little hungry. A turkey on wheat sounds wonderful. Mustard, no mayo."

"A turkey on wheat coming up." Kyle slid from the booth, headed toward the bar and placed a call to the deli, adding a side of fruit salad, a bag of chips and two sodas to the order.

While they waited for lunch, Kyle helped Jade gather up her catalogs and sample books, and carried them to the trunk of her little car. Their sandwiches arrived, and Kyle laid out the spread of food on the bar. They sat side by side on the bar stools and ate.

"You know, I think those new stained glass lamps you ordered to put over the pool tables are going to look wonderful." She looked very pleased with herself since they had been her suggestion. Licking a smear of mustard from her thumb, she glanced around the place, her mind obviously still on her work. "And I have contractors who will refinish the floors and bar. I'll contact them first thing

Monday. They can come in the mornings, so that way their work doesn't interfere with your evening business."

Kyle nodded in agreement as he swallowed a bite of pastrami. "Great."

"As soon as you get final inspection on the restaurant, we'll get started on the decor." Reaching for the fruit salad, she put a heaping spoonful on her paper plate, then stabbed a piece of strawberry with her fork. "Oh, and I wanted to talk to you about your employees' attire."

He eyed her tentatively, wondering what that fanciful mind of hers was conjuring. "What about it?"

"Well, considering all the changes you'll be making, and the classier image you want to project for the bar and restaurant, your employees ought to reflect that image with new uniforms."

The word *uniform* made him shudder. "I don't know. Uniforms remind me of the military, and the years I had to conform to a specific dress code. I'm not sure I want to put myself, or my employees through that."

She rolled her eyes at his resistance. "You don't have to get anything fancy or restricting, but once you refurbish the place you'll need something dressier than jeans and a T-shirt."

He braced his elbows on the bar surface, taking her idea into consideration, as he had all her suggestions. The Black Sheep's current attire was informal and reflected what the bar was now, a casual, laid-back hangout. Though he wanted to maintain that comfortable, easy atmosphere, his main goal was to draw a more expansive range of people to the establishment, and build a clientele that ranged from the middle class to the wealthier population of Santa Monica. He supposed his employees' uniforms ought to exemplify the standard he wanted to create for The Black Sheep.

He glanced at her, meeting her gaze, a part of him still uncertain. "What do you suggest?"

"Well..." She drew the word out, giving him the impression she'd had her strategy figured out long before this moment. "I was thinking of something along the lines of black trousers and a white linen shirt for both the men and women, and a hunter green tie with the name The Black Sheep imprinted on it. And the guys could wear black suspenders. If you want, you could put the bar waitresses in those shorts that actually look like skirts."

"I like it," he said, meaning it. "Simple, practical, but sophisticated."

"Exactly." She flashed him a grin and popped a melon ball into her mouth and chewed. "And you could even—"

Kyle placed his fingers over her soft lips, muffling the rest of her words. "You know, I thought we were done talking business."

She pulled his hand away from her mouth, a sudden awareness leaping to life in her eyes. "Just making good use of our time together."

"I can think of a hundred other ways to make good use of our time together." He smiled slowly and turned on his bar stool so he was facing her. The hand she'd captured lifted again, and he drifted his fingers along her cheek, into her silky hair, and cupped the back of her head. "And plenty of ways to keep that mouth of yours busy."

Her lashes swept downward slumberously, and as he drew her mouth toward his, her lips parted on a welcoming sigh. The easy way she yielded made his blood heat and desire coil deep in his belly. He didn't think she'd admit it, to herself and certainly not to him, but she was beginning to trust him. He could feel it in the flow of her body toward his, and her willingness to let him take the lead.

His lips brushed fleetingly over hers, tempting and soft, a prelim of better things to come. Needing a deeper taste, he gently tilted her head with the pressure of his hand, but before he could settle his mouth over hers, the phone rang.

She jerked back, her eyes opening. A startled look passed over her features.

A growl of disappointment rumbled in his chest. He pulled back so he could look in her dark, golden eyes, but he didn't let her go. "As much as I'd like to ignore whoever is on that phone to kiss you, it might be important." He didn't get many calls on Saturdays, but considering the construction he had underway and the permits he was still trying to obtain, it was possible an inspector was trying to locate him.

She dragged her tongue across her bottom lip, the gesture utterly feminine. "Yeah, you're probably right," she said, her voice husky.

He dipped his head and nibbled on the lower lip she'd just dampened, and she boldly nipped back. The phone rang insistently, and he groaned deeply, in regret, and with a fierce need he was hard-pressed to ignore. "Damn." He forced himself to pull his hand from her hair and slide from his bar stool. "Hold that thought for me, tiger."

Amusement danced in her eyes. "It was your thought, not mine."

The sensual, sassy smile curving her mouth nearly made him say to hell with the call, but he showed incredible restraint and headed to the opposite side of the bar where the phone jingled again. "Hold it anyway, not that I'm likely to forget where we left off."

Jade laughed, not doubting Kyle's claim. She watched him pick up the receiver and slip into the capacity of professional businessman, a role she respected and understood. In less than a minute he was engrossed in his conversation, the words *permits*, *fees* and *inspections* filtering her way.

Knowing he'd be on the phone for a while, she started cleaning up the remnants of their lunch, not minding the chore because it took her mind off the tingling sensation still thrumming through her body.

She cast a quick glance Kyle's way as she stacked their paper plates, thinking how easy he was to like, and just as easy to get along with. He was even proving to be a good friend, something he'd tried establishing six months previously, but she'd been too stubborn and too scared to accept.

She still had a few reservations about their relationship, but those hesitations had little to do with the man she was seeing, but revolved around her own insecurities. After last night she'd seen that, while Kyle was a big flirt, he seemed to be a one-woman man, as he'd stated. She'd seen the women that had flocked around him, trying to attract his attention, and though he'd been amiable, the friendliness hadn't gone beyond the charm of a bartender.

Once the bar was cleared, and the trash tossed into the bin behind the service area, Jade wandered around the lounge, then into the gaming area. She tried her hand at darts, and missed every shot, lodging the sharp, flanged game pieces into the wall on either side of the dart board. Grimacing at her lack of skill and horrible aim, she moved on to the pool tables.

She'd never played pool in her entire life, and she idly wondered if Kyle preferred women more sports-inclined, someone he could play a challenging game of darts or pool with.

Glancing back at Kyle, and finding him still engrossed

in his conversation, she chose a cue stick from a rack on the wall, then began retrieving the balls from a compartment at the end of the pool table. She put the assortment of striped and solid-colored balls on the felt table, letting them roll where they may.

She knew enough to use the solid white ball to hit the other more colorful ones into the corner and side pockets. Leaning over the table, and lining the tip of her stick with the white ball, she drew back and snapped the stick forward. The tip cracked against the white ball with such jarring impact it bounced four times, missing every ball in its path.

She cringed at her pathetic first attempt. Amused laughter erupted behind her, echoing with husky, masculine undertones. She immediately looked over her shoulder, finding Kyle resting his cute rear end on the edge of the other pool table, arms crossed over his chest. How long had he been watching her? She glared, hating the slow heat creeping along her cheeks.

She straightened, and he pushed off his seat and walked toward her, unaffected by her narrow-eyed scowl. "Looks like you're in dire need of some lessons," he said with an easy smile. "Here, let me show you."

The sudden gleam in his eyes, the pure, wicked intent, should have been enough to warn her that his idea of "lessons" was vastly different from her own. But she wasn't about to back down from the challenge, wasn't about to let him think she couldn't handle whatever he decided to dish out.

She sustained her bravado until he turned her back around to face the pool table and his big, warm body crowded her from behind. Her heart raced, and she knew she was in big trouble...like the midnight swim at the pool, like the evening in his office with the peaches.

He reached around her and grabbed the cue stick, positioning it in her hands the proper way. "Now align the tip of the cue stick about two inches away from the cue ball, which is that solid white ball."

Okay, nothing illicit about that, she thought. She leaned over the table to do as he instructed, and became too aware of just how close he stood. Her bottom brushed across the front of his jeans, and coarse denim scratched the back of her bare thighs. She swallowed hard and focused on that damned white ball, determined to ignore the desire slowly unraveling within her.

"Your form is all wrong," he chided, his voice a smoky, sexy murmur. "Don't round your back so much." Placing his hand at her nape, he slowly dragged his palm down to the base of her spine, softening her posture. A purring sound rolled into her throat, and she promptly swallowed it. Her senses spun wildly, making concentrating on the game nearly impossible.

He placed his hands on her hips, his touch so hot, their position so suggestive, she couldn't breathe, couldn't think. "Now relax, take aim, and give it your best shot," he said.

Her best shot missed the white ball completely. The tip of her stick scratched the felt surface with such force she expected the fabric to rip. In frustration and exasperation, she dropped the stick and straightened to turn around, but Kyle's arms were suddenly around her waist, preventing her from escaping a situation that had suddenly turned intimate and very threatening.

She resisted the frantic urge to pry his hands from her. "I don't think pool is my kind of game," she said tersely.

He didn't release her, as her tone demanded. Instead, in his usual bold manner, he touched his mouth to her ear and murmured, "Then let's play another game. One we can both learn together."

Suppressing a shiver, she closed her eyes. But the images of the kind of game he wanted to play were so vivid, so arousing, she immediately blinked her lashes back open. Damn him, he'd changed the rules on her, using their situation to seduce her. And her body was falling for the scheme, wanting him with an insane, instantaneous hunger she was powerless to resist.

Feeling a surge of panic and needing space, she placed her hands over his to pull them away. He caught her fingers, entwining them in between his and held her hostage. She pulled in a deep breath that did nothing to steady her erratic heartbeat. "Kyle, I don't think this is such a good idea."

"Whenever we get close and intimate, you always fall back on that excuse." His tone was lazy, but the tension radiating from his body was anything but relaxed. "What are you afraid of, Jade?"

The answer to his question came all too easily, and for some odd reason, not looking him in the eye made it easier to blurt out the truth. "Of falling for you."

"Would that be such a bad thing?" He sounded genuinely perplexed.

"Yes," she whispered fiercely.

He was quiet for a moment, cradling her gently in his embrace, the heat and strength of him seeping into her skin. His body was so still, she could feel the heavy beating of his heart against her back. She wondered if she'd finally managed to make him realize what he was up against—a haunting, painful past that kept her from giving her heart to any man. Including him. Lord knew every time he tried to get close she did her best to push him away.

She expected him to let her go, but he didn't. At the very least she expected him to be annoyed—what kind of man would put up with such an ego-damaging answer?—but she detected no animosity.

Instead, in a soft, soothing voice, he summed up her biggest fear. "You don't trust easily, do you?"

"People take advantage of trust," she snapped, feeling emotionally defensive and physically trapped.

"Some people do," he agreed, stroking his thumbs over the back of her hands, the gesture calming her. "And you think I'm one of those people."

She hated the way that sounded. She'd known him for six months, and not once had he given her any indication that he'd take advantage of her, control her or methodically steal her self-confidence until she was nothing but a shell of herself. If anything, these past weeks with him had bolstered her, giving her a self-assurance and sensual awareness of herself that radiated from the inside out.

She was confused and torn. "I don't know anymore," she said, her throat tight and aching.

"I'm not like that," he promised. "I'd never deliberately hurt you, Jade. But you'll have to trust my word and me. Can you do that?"

No! The instinctive, protective answer screamed in her mind. The last man she'd been so naive as to trust had taken advantage of it, using that trust to manipulate her emotions and nearly destroying her in the process. She wouldn't, *couldn't*, allow herself to make that same mistake with Kyle. Her self-preservation and emotional well-being depended on it.

"I want to touch you," he said, his rich, deep voice hypnotic and cajoling. "Will you let me?"

"Kyle, this is all happening so fast." Yet not fast enough, she thought, unable to stop the currents of excitement racing through her. The thrill was real, as real and hot as the man behind her.

"We won't do anything you don't want to." He seemed to know and understand her fears, catering to them in a way no one but her imaginary lover ever had. "We'll go only as far as you let me. Just say stop, at any time, and I will."

Jade bit her bottom lip, debating. She wanted this. She feared it, but she knew she would forever regret letting this moment slip away.

"Okay," she whispered, her voice holding a slight quiver.

Releasing her, he swept the striped and solid balls to the far side of the pool table. They clicked together and rolled into the pockets, leaving the surface clear. He then braced his hands on the rim of the table, keeping her secured in the circle of his arms. "Put your hands on the table, and keep them there."

She hesitated, the familiarity of his request startling her. She remembered a similar demand, a cool stone wall and the scent of roses. Even as her mind struggled between an illusion she'd created on paper and reality, her body thrummed in anticipation.

Before she lost her nerve, she bent forward and placed her flattened palms on the soft, felt surface. With Kyle's thighs bracketing hers from behind, and his pelvis snug against her bottom, she felt defenseless.

She turned her head, looking over her shoulder, meeting dark blue eyes glinting with something a little untamed. "Kyle?"

He leaned his body over hers, claiming her with breath-stealing intimacy. His hands covered hers on the table, and he skimmed his lips along her cheek. "Ready to stop so soon?"

The fantasy was so tangible, the man behind her so vibrant and real, she didn't want it to slip away. Closing her eyes, she shook her head. "No, don't stop."

She felt him smile against her neck. "Good."

His palms glided up her braced arms, his fingers feathering into her armpits until she squirmed and shivered at the tickling sensation. His touch was innocent and light, until he came to the buttons securing the front of her silky camisole. His fingers worked the buttons through the loops with an impatience that had her breasts swelling in her bra, and her breathing deepening. The urgency grew, in her and him—she could feel the thick ridge of his erection straining against her bottom—until she half expected him to rip her top open. Almost wanted him to.

But he didn't. Once the front hung open, he unclasped her lacy bra and let her full breasts sway forward. Her nipples tightened, and she curled her fingers into fists against the table, waiting for him to fill his palms, to caress her.

"Touch me," she urged, barely believing she'd spoken the words in her mind aloud. But she had—his soft, masculine chuckles confirmed it—and she didn't regret them, especially when he obliged and cupped her breasts in his large palms, kneading the fullness while his fingers grazed over the crested tips.

The heaviness in her intensified, spiraling downward. Seemingly knowing what she wanted, what she needed, his hands moved on, sliding down her ribs, over the waistband of her skirt, until his palms grazed her bare thighs. He didn't linger, but she didn't want him to. He pushed the hem of her skirt up, dragging the denim over the curve of her hip and waist, until her wispy peach panties and his jeans were the only thing separating them.

He wedged a boot between her sandaled feet, making

her legs move apart for him. His hands returned to her thighs, drawing swirling patterns with his fingers and leisurely drifting up the inside of her quivering legs. He murmured gentle, coaxing words of encouragement in her ear, told her how beautiful she was, and how much he wanted her.

She melted with each caress of his hands and mouth on her skin. Idly, she wondered why she was so helpless to resist him, when she'd resisted every man in the past three years who'd tried to get close. Kyle had a way of weakening her defenses and tapping into her most intimate longings, making her want all the things she'd denied herself for so long, the flesh-and-blood touch of a man, the feeling of being cherished and desired....

He was becoming the perfect fantasy lover, in her mind and in reality.

His thumbs traced the crease where her thighs gave way to her most intimate place, while his mouth trailed hot, damp kisses along her neck. She felt alive, impatient and so aroused she shamelessly pressed her bottom more urgently against his pelvis. In response, he splayed a hand low on her belly and rolled his hips forward in an erotic, reckless rhythm. And then he gently sank his teeth into the curve of her neck and shoulder.

Jade's entire body arched, and her breath caught sharply at the electric sensations rippling along her nerve endings. She tried to turn, but he wouldn't let her—she didn't stand a chance against the powerful, muscular thighs and the strength and width of his chest holding her captive.

Before she had a chance to recover from that passionate, primitive assault, he wrapped an arm around her waist, and with his other hand slipped his fingers beneath the elastic band of her panties. He touched damp curls and found the heated core of her.

She whimpered and began to tremble. She went a little bit crazy, and a whole lot wild, forgetting caution or reason for the all-consuming pleasure his slow, insidious touch evoked. "Please." The word escaped her before she could stop it.

He pulled her tighter against him, his teeth and tongue grazing her jaw, her neck, her shoulder. "Oh, God, Jade," he groaned into her ear. "You're so warm, so soft...*so wet.*"

His blatantly erotic words, the skill of his fingers ruthlessly stroking, sliding persuasively, then slipping intimately, deeply, into her body sent her soaring. She came on a soft, keening cry. Her entire body convulsed with the wondrous, voluptuous pleasure, her head rolled back to his shoulder.

She trembled in the aftermath, the intensity of her orgasm stunning her. The way he wrapped both arms around her when it was over comforted her. The words he whispered in her ear were sweet and endearing.

She waited as her heart rate slowed, fully expecting him to take their foreplay to its logical conclusion. And even though she wasn't completely certain she was ready for that ultimate act of intimacy with him, she knew she wouldn't stop him, either.

But once again he seemed to sense her doubts. He eased her skirt back down her hips and gently turned her around to hook her bra and button her camisole. She let him tend to her disheveled clothing, baffled by his restraint. He had every opportunity to take advantage of their very erotic situation, but the fact that he'd held his own raging desires in check was proof that she *could* trust him.

The prospect wasn't as scary as it once had been.

Kyle finished with the buttons on Jade's blouse and finally risked a glance at her face, which was still flushed with passion. Supreme satisfaction filled him, making his own sacrifice worth what he'd gained. Her confidence in him.

She pulled in a steady breath, looking slightly embarrassed. "That was very one-sided."

"I'm not complaining, tiger. I thoroughly enjoyed myself, and you." He dragged his thumb across her bottom lip, regretting that he hadn't had the opportunity to spend more time kissing her. He loved her mouth, the soft texture, the honeyed taste, and the silky heat inside. "You're an incredibly sexy woman."

Her face flushed a deeper shade of pink, but she didn't shy away from him or his light caresses. "But what about you?"

He grinned. "I'm a patient fellow." Though he couldn't ignore that he was still rock hard and more than willing. "As much as I want you, this isn't how I want our first time together to be. When we make love, the time and place needs to be as special as you are."

Her expression softened, and she gave him a sultry, teasing smile. "You'd better be careful, or I could really fall for you."

He knew she was just humoring him, but he was surprised to realize how much he liked the way that sounded. How much he wanted it to be true. "I'm counting on it, tiger."

SHE COULDN'T CONCENTRATE, and it was all Kyle's fault.

Knowing it was futile to continue working on the fabric and tile order for the Briar Estates account Casual Elegance had recently acquired, she closed her invoice book and put the file into her briefcase to take back to work tomorrow.

So much for bringing work home to get ahead on orders. It was too quiet in her guest bedroom-makeshift office, and there weren't the continual interruptions and distractions the office provided to keep her so busy that thoughts of Kyle couldn't intrude.

Ever since their encounter at The Black Sheep four days ago, he'd occupied her thoughts during idle times, as did the fact that he'd managed to seduce her on three separate occasions. And every time, usually in some subtle, obscure way, their encounters had reminded her of old fantasies she'd written.

She was certain her mind was playing tricks on her. After three years of being alone and sharing intimacies with a fantasy lover, her subconscious was accepting those fantasies as reality.

It was the only explanation that made sense.

So why was it when she closed her eyes and thought of the fantasy lover she'd created she no longer saw his face, but Kyle's instead? It was as if the two were merging, illusion evolving into a flesh-and-blood man who made her feel real emotions she hadn't allowed herself to contemplate outside of her fantasies—passion, desire, need. And most important, with Kyle's easy persuasion, she was gaining confidence in herself as a woman and lover.

She was beginning to trust him, and her own judgment of him.

Desk cleared and files and sample books put away, she snapped off the old, antique lamp and left the office. With the thought of her old journal of fantasies on her mind, she headed toward her bedroom in search of the book, curious to see how similar those fantasies were to the three episodes with Kyle.

It had been over a year since she'd started writing in her sapphire blue journal, and she couldn't remember where she'd last seen the burgundy one. She checked all the obvious places: in her nightstand drawers, in her dresser drawers, and rummaged through the floral boxes on the top shelf of her walk-in closet where she stashed personal stuff.

Nothing.

Thinking she'd possibly misplaced it when she'd bought her new bedroom furniture, she continued her pursuit, looking in conspicuous places and not-so-obvious nooks and crannies. Her search included the guest bedroom-office, where she kept trade books in a walnut case, and the new hutch in her living room.

The burgundy journal was nowhere to be found.

7

JADE TURNED HER Mazda Miata into her parents' circular drive and parked behind Grey and Mariah's Jeep Cherokee. She killed the engine, but made no move to exit. She stared out the windshield at the big house she'd been raised in, a house where she and her sister had shared so many hopes and dreams for their future.

At least her sister's dreams of having a husband and family had come true. Hers had been shattered three years ago. She shuddered to think where she'd be now if she hadn't come to her senses and ended her relationship with Adam. If she hadn't had the support of her family who'd helped her through the most devastating period in her life.

"Are you sure you're okay with me being here today?"

Jade blinked away her thoughts and glanced toward the passenger side of the car, where Kyle had folded his large frame into the compact seat of her sports car. Despite the cramped quarters, he hadn't once complained that he couldn't stretch out his long legs, or that the top of his head nearly hit the ceiling of the car.

Although he'd provided her an out, she'd decided there was absolutely nothing wrong with bringing a male friend to her birthday barbecue. Besides, she wanted him there. It was her parents' problem if they made more of her relationship with Kyle than there actually was.

She pulled her key from the ignition, her mouth lifting

in a wry smile. "How can you expect me to be sure of anything? I'm thirty years old today."

Reaching across the console, he sifted his fingers through her short hair, his gaze full of the teasing charm she was coming to adore. "If it makes you feel any better, you don't look a day over twenty-one."

She couldn't contain her light laughter, nor could she help the special way he made her feel, all from a touch and a few words. "You're a wonderful liar, but it does make me feel better. I hope you're still around when I hit forty."

He lifted a brow. "Do you think I plan on going somewhere?"

His question didn't really require an answer, because she knew what he meant. And as much as Kyle being a permanent part of her life was beginning to appeal to her, she knew their versions of "permanent" differed vastly. For him, it meant that they'd be friends months and years from now, long after their affair ended, but they'd each have their own separate lives that didn't include each other on a regular basis. No commitment, no ties, no obligation to the other.

Her chest tightened, right in the vicinity of her heart. Oh, Lord, when had all those emotional connections started to matter? And when had having an affair with Kyle begun to have a deeper meaning than an outlet for her attraction to the man? They hadn't even slept together, and already she was falling deeper than was wise.

"Jade!"

Welcoming the diversion from her wayward thoughts, Jade glanced to the front of the house. Mariah waved and walked down the front steps, her soft, floral dress swirling around her legs. Kayla, perched on her mother's hip, imitated her mother and waved, too. Grey followed at a more leisurely pace, then her parents filled the doorway, no doubt anxious to meet her guest.

"Looks like the troops are closing in." She grabbed her purse and took a deep, fortifying breath. "As much as I'd like to spend the day drowning my woes in a half gallon carton of Rocky Road, my family refuses to let this day pass uncelebrated."

Kyle's deep, rich chuckles filled the small confines of her car. "I'll do whatever I can to make the transition from the twenties to thirties as painless as possible."

She gave him a grateful smile as they exited the car and headed toward the house. They walked side by side, and she deliberately kept her purse in the hand brushing his so he wouldn't attempt to hold her hand and give her family the impression they were an item. But that didn't dissuade the rogue from touching her, and giving their avid audience something to speculate on.

He lightly splayed his fingers on her back, bare from the backless teal blue halter short set she'd worn. An instantaneous heat and electric awareness flared within her, making her breath catch in her throat and her breasts swell in shameless abandon. Her body's complimentary response to his no longer shocked her; it excited her beyond anything she'd ever experienced.

It had been a week since the morning at The Black Sheep, and they hadn't had any quality time alone this past week because they'd both been busy with their hectic and conflicting schedules—hers during the day, his at night. But that hadn't stopped Kyle from taking advantage of every moment they did seem to find together, no matter how brief. Whether it was in passing in the lobby when she came home from work and he left for the bar, or a brief visit from him in the morning or during her lunch hour. In the span of seconds, he drove her crazy with one of his deep, silky kisses, or a bold caress that left her wanting more. And his phone calls always seemed to take a provocative turn, as well.

The building anticipation was driving her crazy!

Mariah met them first and wrapped Jade in a hug that made Kayla squeal in delight.

"Happy birthday, sis," she said, then welcomed Kyle into the fold with a brief, warm embrace, which, Jade knew, was her way of stating she fully approved of Kyle.

Grey gave Jade a hug, too. When he pulled back, his dark brown eyes were filled with feigned shock. "Ohmigod! Are those wrinkles I see around your eyes?"

Jade shot Mariah a dark look. Obviously her loving sister had told Grey she was going into the next decade kicking and screaming, and he was taking advantage of the situation. She'd grown fond of her brother-in-law since he'd made an honest woman out of her sister, not that she'd ever admit that to *him*.

Lifting her fist, she playfully cuffed Grey on the chin. "You'd better watch yourself, Nichols, I'm not so old that I can't put a few wrinkles on that handsome face of yours."

He grinned. "And here I thought you'd mellow with age." Before she could summon a response to that smart remark, he extended his hand toward Kyle and introduced himself. "I'm Grey, Mariah's husband."

Kyle shook his hand. "Kyle Stephens. It's a pleasure to meet you."

Grey nodded toward Jade, a devilish grin touching his lips. "Maybe you'll have better luck mellowing her."

"Oh, I don't know," he said, meeting Jade's gaze, and giving her a slow wink filled with all sorts of wicked insinuations. "I happen to like her just the way she is."

Grey shook his dark head, oblivious to the sexual undercurrents sparking between them. "You're a braver man than most."

Kyle merely smiled that winning smile of his, and Jade had the thought that most men weren't as *persistent* as Kyle. And not nearly so patient and understanding of her needs and fears.

They continued up to the porch, where she introduced Kyle to her parents, Jim and Donna, as a friend and a Casual Elegance client. Her mother was her usual sweet, courteous self, though there was a fair amount of curiosity sparkling in her blue eyes. Her father openly sized Kyle up while shaking his hand. To Jade's relief, they got through introductions with a minimum of embarrassment and not one question about Kyle's intentions.

But that didn't mean her father wouldn't take advantage of an opportune moment later.

They all headed to the backyard, where her father had the barbecue heating up. Her mother brought out marinated chicken and ribs, issued instructions for Jim to start cooking the meat, then told Jade and Mariah that she needed their help getting the outside table set, and the side dishes out.

"Will you be okay?" Jade asked Kyle, casting a surreptitious glance at her father, who was behaving himself so far.

Grey handed Kyle a cold beer and grinned at her. "Don't worry about Kyle, he'll be just fine. I'm sure we can find *something* to talk about."

"That's what I'm afraid of," she muttered, and gave her brother-in-law a warning look. "Behave yourself, Nichols, or there will be hell to pay later."

He chuckled, having been on the receiving end of her version of hell. "I don't doubt that in the least."

As she walked across the covered patio, she heard Kyle

say to Grey, "Jade tells me you're in the security business. With the new restaurant coming in, I've been thinking of updating the current security system I have. What can you suggest?"

Knowing business would keep the boys distracted for a while, Jade slipped inside the cool house. She walked into the kitchen, where her mother was mixing the potato salad. A smorgasbord of food lined the counter, enough to feed an army. Her mother always enjoyed their family get-togethers and usually went all out in the food department, trying to make everyone's favorites.

Donna rinsed her hands in the sink, her gaze traveling out the kitchen window to the backyard. It wasn't hard to figure who she was looking at. "Kyle seems like a nice man," she commented.

Snagging a carrot stick from the relish tray, she dipped it into the accompanying ranch dressing. "He's very nice, Mom."

Donna glanced over her shoulder at her, the speculation Jade had been waiting for bright in her mother's gaze. "Is it serious between you two?"

Jade munched on her carrot. She supposed it depended on one's version of serious. Their attraction was as serious as anything she'd ever experienced—intense and hot. But there were no promises between them, no deep, lasting commitment. Kyle was a rebel, a maverick, a man who lived for the moment. And at the moment, she was what he lived for.

"He's just a friend," Mariah offered as she came into the kitchen from the adjoining family room, where she'd put Kayla down for a nap. "Or at least that's what Jade tells me."

"He's a friend and a client," she confirmed.

"A client you're dating," Mariah added.

They hadn't managed to go out on a date yet, but she didn't bother to argue the point with Mariah. Instead, she just rolled her eyes, and prayed that Kyle wasn't receiving the same interrogation. Picking up the Crock-Pot of baked beans, she headed back outside. Mariah followed with plates and silverware, then went back for napkins and glasses.

As she and Mariah set the table, Jade glanced toward the barbecue where her father, Grey and Kyle were engrossed in conversation. Knowing the guys were out of earshot, she gathered the courage to ask her sister a question that had been bothering her for nearly a week now.

She drew a deep breath, and released it, along with her sister's name. "Mariah?"

Her sister looked up from the napkin she was folding and smiled. "Yes?"

As casually as she could manage, she asked, "Remember when you were helping me put things out for the yard sale last month?"

Mariah nodded.

"Well, you didn't happen to come across a journal, did you?"

There was no sign of recognition on Mariah's face. "What kind of journal?"

A book of intimate fantasies and her most private, secret desires. "A personal journal," she said, keeping her description vague. "It's about half-an-inch thick and has a burgundy cover."

Mariah thought for a moment. "I can't say that I did. Besides, I didn't go through your personal things."

"I didn't mean it that way." She put a fork and knife at each setting. "I can't find it and thought maybe you'd seen it when you were taking those books out of the old headboard."

"Not that I can recall." She tilted her head, and her silky blond hair swung over her shoulder. "Where did you put it last?"

Mariah's practical question sparked a bit of annoyance. "If I remembered, I wouldn't be asking if you saw it, now would I?"

"Geez, you don't have to get so sensitive about it," Mariah replied in a droll tone. "It's just a book."

Not just *any* book, she wanted to refute, but kept her mouth shut, unwilling to share something so personal. Even with her sister.

"It has to be somewhere," Mariah went on. "How many times have you stashed away something personal or important then couldn't remember where you'd put it?"

Mariah knew her faults too well. "Too many times to count," she admitted reluctantly.

"It's not like you're the most organized person in the family," Mariah pointed out, then soothed that sibling wisecrack with a little reassurance. "I'm sure when you least expect it, you'll come across your journal."

She sighed. "You're probably right."

Mariah grinned broadly. "About you being disorganized, or eventually finding the book?"

Jade couldn't contain a sheepish grin. "Both."

A teasing light shone in Mariah's eyes. "You know, I kind of like it when you admit to your faults."

Jade feigned indignation. "I did no such thing!"

Mariah just smiled and sauntered back toward the sliding door leading into the kitchen to bring out more side dishes.

Before long the six of them were seated at the outdoor table, enjoying the warm summer day, and the spread of food. Jade got her share of good-natured ribbing about being over-the-hill, and her father regaled Kyle with amusing, and sometimes embarrassing, tales of when she and Mariah were growing up. They talked about Kyle's new restaurant, and the time he'd spent in the marines.

The only topic Kyle didn't seem willing to elaborate on when asked by her father was his family. Knowing a little about the dissension between him and his father and brother, she understood his reluctance. He kept his comments light and superficial, though she could see how uncomfortable he was with the subject.

Everybody liked Kyle, which didn't really surprise Jade. He was so easy to get along with.

It was too bad he wasn't going to be around in the future.

And why did that thought bother her so much?

"I HAD A GREAT TIME today," Kyle said as they drove back to their complex. Since it was only a little after six, Kyle planned on using the rest of the evening for their own *private*, birthday party. "Thanks for inviting me."

Taking her gaze off the road for a few seconds, she gave him a dubious smile, though she looked totally relaxed. "If I remember correctly, I think it was my sister who invited you, but I'm glad you came along."

"You've got a great family." And he had to admit he was a little envious of the closeness they all shared, something he'd never experienced with his own family. Much to his pleasure, everyone today had made him feel a part of the fold, accepting him unconditionally. It had been wonderful to be in a family setting without having to face the issues of what a rough and rebellious kid he'd been, and what a disappointment he was to his family.

There had been no one's expectations to live up to today. He'd set his own standards, and had been accepted for who and what he was: a bartender and restaurant owner. He liked that. A whole lot.

"Yeah, they're not so bad," Jade said as she switched lanes on the freeway to exit. "Did my father grill you too much?"

"Nothing I couldn't handle. He was just concerned that I didn't hurt his little girl."

She cringed. "I'm not so little anymore."

"No, but since I'm the first guy you've brought home since Adam, I suppose he was a little concerned about who his daughter was getting involved with."

Her head snapped around as she coasted down the off-ramp. "My father told you about Adam?"

The combination of incredulity and anger in her voice was enough to tell him he was treading on very sensitive territory. He'd finally been given a few clues to Jade's reserve, her apprehension toward him and their developing relationship, and he wasn't above exploiting them. "Actually, Grey mentioned him. From what Mariah has told him, he said the guy was a real bastard."

Her face flushed. "What else did he say?" she asked tightly.

"That the details of the relationship should probably come from you."

She applied the brakes at the stoplight with enough force to make his seat belt tighten against his chest. "He was a jerk," she said succinctly, as if that were the only detail he needed to know.

He'd gathered as much, but he wanted, suddenly needed, to know how this man had had such a detrimental effect on Jade, to the point that she would avoid any involvement with a man for nearly three years. "Want to tell me about it?"

Her fingers tightened on the steering wheel, and when

her teal blue gaze met his, he saw a glimpse of pain and apprehension that grabbed at something elemental in him. She'd been hurt very badly.

"There's not much to tell." Her tone was brusque, tinged with a lingering bitterness. "We dated. He had a thing about control. I fell into the trap. A humiliating experience made me see the light. End of relationship. End of story."

He gathered it had also been the end to her trust in men. She'd created a fantasy lover whom *she* had complete control over. She dictated the level of intimacy, and played it safe by stopping short of making love.

The light turned green, and she pressed on the accelerator, continuing steadily down the street. She blew out a long breath, and her tense shoulders sagged. "I'm sorry," she said quietly. "Getting through my thirtieth birthday is bad enough. I don't want to ruin the rest of the evening talking about my relationship with Adam."

He guessed she didn't want to talk about Adam at all. He'd give her a reprieve for now. "Fair enough. I haven't given you your birthday present yet. It's at my place."

She turned into the driveway leading to their complex and parked her car in her spot. "You didn't have to get me anything."

He smiled. After sharing her with her family today, and not spending much time with her during the week, he was anxious to be alone with her. "I wanted to."

They got out of the car, and he tucked her hand in his, gratified when she curled her fingers around his. Once they were inside his condo, he left her in the living room and went into the bedroom to get her gift. The phone rang just as he reached his dresser, where he'd put her present, wrapped in pink paper and topped with a frilly bow.

He only had one phone, a cordless unit with a built-in

answering machine, which he kept in the living room. "Would you mind grabbing that?" he called to Jade, since she was closer. "I'll be there in a sec."

"Sure." Before the next ring he heard a beep as she connected the line, and her soft answer, "Hello?"

He rounded the corner from the bedroom back into the living room, her gift in hand, just as she said, "No, you've got the right number." She paused for a second, listening, then said, "Hold on, he's right here."

A slight smile curved her mouth as she handed over the cordless phone. "It's your daughter."

Setting the flat, square wrapped box on the coffee table, he took the phone from Jade, thinking his offspring had impeccable timing, though he never minded hearing from her. "Hi, sweetheart. How are you?"

"Dad!" she exclaimed excitedly. "I can't believe a woman answered your phone. Does that mean you actually have a girlfriend?"

He'd consider Jade at least that. He *was* seeing her exclusively. "Yes, is that okay with you?"

"It's more than okay." Her spirited teenage voice sounded almost giddy. "Is it serious?"

He glanced at Jade, who'd settled herself at the far end of the couch. He'd dated many women through the years, but none of them had ever stimulated or excited him the way Jade did, to the extent that he wanted no one but her. "Yes, I believe it is."

"It's about time, Dad! God, I never thought you'd settle down. When are you getting married? I want to be there when you tie the knot."

He grimaced over his daughter's enthusiasm. "Whoa, Christy, who said anything about marriage?"

Jade met his gaze, her brows raised in question. He

gave a helpless shrug that hopefully conveyed he had nothing to do with his daughter's meddling.

"Dad, you need to settle down and get married. Mom even thinks so, too."

"She does, does she?" he asked, though he'd heard a subtle lecture or two from Jamie Ann about the benefits of marriage.

More quietly, Christy added, "I worry about you, and I hate the thought of you being all alone, with no family around."

His daughter was way too wise for her years. He'd been without a family for so long, he'd sworn he was better off without one. After spending time with Jade's family today, he was beginning to realize what he'd never had with his own family—the support, the laughter, the love—and what he'd given up when he and Jamie Ann had made the decision not to get married—the chance to have a family of his own. The regret hit harder than usual, surprising him.

"You know I always love to hear from you, Christy," he said, steering their conversation back to neutral territory. "But I'm assuming you didn't call to exult my love life."

"Well, no," she said a bit sheepishly. "Actually, I told you a couple of months ago that I was looking around for a car to buy. Well, I found one. It's a used Camaro, and it's really cool."

"I'll bet it is," he muttered, imagining the guys that would be eyeing the sporty car and the beautiful young woman behind the wheel. It was enough to give him an ulcer, because he knew exactly what those young bucks would be thinking.

He shook off those unsettling thoughts. "I told you I'd help you buy a car as soon as you found one your mother and Tony approved of," he agreed, "but do you think we can discuss this later? Like maybe tomorrow?"

"Oh, absolutely," she said, giving in too easily. "I *totally* understand that you're busy right now."

That worried him. What did his daughter know of his kind of busy?

They said goodbye, and he shook his head as he disconnected the line and slipped the phone back in the unit. He walked to the sliding door leading to the balcony, opened it, and stood there, staring out at the evening shadows darkening the courtyard.

"I swear that child is growing up way too fast," he said, more to himself than Jade. Seventeen years—from her first tooth, through ballet recitals, and now, to her first car—gone. All without him being there to share in the most important years of her life. That fact troubled him the most, but it had been the right and only choice during such a tumultuous time in his life. Some days, though, it didn't feel so right.

Some days, it hurt like hell.

"You miss her, don't you?" Jade asked softly from behind him.

He dragged his hand through his hair, suddenly feeling much older than his thirty-five years. "Yeah, I do. Sporadic visits and phone calls aren't nearly enough." They never had been, but he'd always told himself that it was better this way. That his daughter was better off with Jamie Ann and Tony. And when she'd been a toddler, that was probably the truth. He'd been such a rebel, so determined *not* to be what his father expected of him, that he was certain he wouldn't have been the kind of father Christy needed. One she could have depended on. One who'd put her needs before his own.

He couldn't help wondering if things wouldn't have

turned out differently had Christy been born later, when he hadn't been so hardheaded and such a wild hellion out to defy his father. If maybe he'd be living in a suburb somewhere with a wife and 2.5 children, instead of convincing himself he was cut out to be a bachelor and didn't need anyone.

It was a sobering thought.

Jade leaned against the wall next to him. "How come you never married Christy's mother?"

He met her gaze, seeing the mild curiosity there. She wasn't judging him, wasn't condemning him for a decision that everyone else had construed as irresponsible.

He'd like to believe that *not* marrying Jamie Ann had been one of the more responsible decisions he'd made.

"Because we both realized it would never work between us. Not in the long run, anyway." He shoved his hands into the front pockets of his jean shorts and transferred his gaze back out to the courtyard, his thoughts going back seventeen years. "We were both so young, and I was so wild and defiant. I would have grown to resent the situation, and we probably would have ended up hating one another. We were both smart enough to take that into consideration, and responsible enough to know the odds were against us. Marriage would have only made matters worse."

Unfortunately, neither of their parents had seen their choice as a responsible one, and had been furious at him for deserting Jamie Ann to join the marines. Though Jamie Ann's parents had long ago forgiven him, his own family hadn't been so benevolent.

"Despite how rough those first few years were for Jamie Ann, things worked out for the best," he said, giving Jade a smile. "She's found a great husband who treats her like a queen, and Christy has a decent father. They both deserve that."

She touched his arm, her fingers a light caress. "You're a good man, Kyle."

He raised a brow. "What makes you say that?"

"Because you care. Because Jamie Ann and Christy are two of the most important people in your life, and you put their happiness above your own."

Her observation stunned him. Did she really understand how difficult it was some days to accept the sacrifice he'd made when he'd left Jamie Ann and Christy? How hard it was to watch his daughter grow up through letters, phone calls and photographs?

"Don't make me into some kind of hero, Jade," he said, more gruffly than he intended. "I'm just fortunate that everything turned out amicably."

"Except with your family."

"That won't change."

"But don't you deserve to be happy, too?"

"Who says I'm not?" he countered, feeling as though she was backing him into an emotional corner.

"I guess you'd know better than anyone," she said.

He frowned. He was satisfied with his life, but he'd be lying if he said there wasn't a certain void he experienced every now and then. An emptiness he'd managed to ignore for more years than he cared to recall.

More and more lately he found himself analyzing where he was in his life, and missing things he wished he had. Things he'd convinced himself he didn't need. He'd believed the bar was enough to be his mistress, the employees and patrons a part of his family, and the new restaurant his baby.

When had that started not being enough?

He looked at the woman beside him, and realized she

filled that void in him, and enhanced his life in a way no other woman ever had. She made him feel worthy. She accepted who he was and the mistakes he'd made. He'd always steered clear of commitment and ties.... So why did he find himself wondering what it would be like to come home to Jade on a daily basis, and make love to her every night?

"What about you, Jade?" he asked, turning the tables on her. "Are you happy?"

Her expression turned cautious. "In certain areas of my life, yes."

"And other areas?"

She knew what he was asking; he could see the reserve in her gaze, the struggle to keep him from prying the truth from her. He was digging past the surface, to emotional wants, needs and desires. Things past the tangible and superficial, to something deeply rooted.

"I don't know," she whispered.

It was as honest as answers got, because he didn't know anymore either.

"You know," he drawled, reaching for her hand and hoping to dispel the serious mood between them, "this isn't the way I'd intended to spend the evening."

"Me, either," she admitted, her voice husky, and her eyes darkening with awareness.

Pulling her back to the couch, he made her sit on the cushion, and settled himself next to her. Then he handed her the small gift. "Open your present."

She hesitated for a moment, then pulled off the bow and tore open the paper. She lifted the flat lid and gasped. Her gaze shot to his, wide with apprehension, and shimmering with a delight she tried to suppress.

Her finger traced the rose pattern on the gold anklet. "Kyle, this is too much."

It was beginning to be not enough. In so many ways. "Do you like it?"

"Of course, but—"

He pressed his fingers over her soft lips, not wanting to hear her protests. "Then I expect you to wear it and enjoy it. Will you do that for me?"

She pulled his hand away, an incredibly soft and sensual smile touching her mouth. "Yes. Will you put it on me?"

He grinned, not about to decline the task. "It would be my pleasure."

And it was. Kneeling in front of her while she sat on the couch, he braced her sandaled foot on his thigh and retrieved the exquisite anklet from the velvet lining. He secured the clasp around her slender ankle, and glanced up as he smoothed a hand over her calf. "It suits you. It goes with your free spirit, and compliments your sassy, sexy personality."

Her face flushed, and she ducked her head to admire her gift, which glinted in the light. "Thank you. I love it."

And I'm falling in love with you. The realization slammed into him from out of left field, causing his heart to thud heavily in his chest. Oh, man...he didn't know if he was ready for this. Didn't know if he could be everything she needed him to be.

Their gazes connected, held suspended on a timeless, sensual moment. Finally he released a long, low breath. "Happy birthday, Jade."

"Oh, Kyle." There was so much emotion in her voice, enough to tell him she was just as affected as he by whatever it was happening between them. She leaned down and brushed her soft, incredibly sexy mouth across his, lightly at first, then pressing deeper. He let his lips part, let her tongue slip inside to stroke along his. The kiss quickly flared out of control, grew demanding and avaricious. She wrapped her fists in his shirt and slowly drew him up between her parted knees.

Groaning deep in his throat, he followed her lead, willing to go anywhere with her. Willing to do anything for her. She only needed to ask, with her mouth, with her hands, with her body.

And she did. Her sweet, hot mouth talked to him as he'd never been talked to before, asking for things he wanted just as much as she. The hands gliding up his shoulders, then tangling in his hair begged for closeness, and her arching body spoke a language as old as time. It was enough to make him spontaneously combust.

She felt the same way, judging by the hot feel of her skin beneath the hands he slowly slid up her thighs. She shuddered and moaned, and broke their kiss to look into his eyes. Her own were a deep, dark shade of green-blue, and he had the sudden, annoying thought that he *still* didn't know what her real eye color was.

But he would, of that he was certain.

Her trembling fingers tightened in his hair. "What are you doing to me?" she whispered.

He knew her question went beyond physical stimulation to more emotional sensations, because he was feeling a little shook up himself. "I'm trying to seduce you." He pressed her back on the couch, moved his body over hers, and caught the dizzying scent of peaches that clung to her. "Is it working yet?"

"Yes," she breathed, her lashes drifting shut as he lowered his head to nuzzle her neck, her shoulder. "Oh, yes..."

The phone rang, and she started beneath him, the obnoxious sound pulling her out of the trance she'd been in. "Kyle?"

"Let the answering machine pick it up." His voice was rough with arousal, his body just as turned on. No way did he want to let this woman out of his arms. Dropping his mouth over hers, he kissed her deeply, shutting out his outgoing message that clicked on in the background.

"Kyle, we're swamped down here," Bruce said, a harried edge to his voice. "If you get this message, we could use an extra hand."

Leaving his employees shorthanded was something Kyle couldn't ignore. Dragging his lips from Jade's eager, pliant ones, he sat up and reached for the cordless phone, muttering, "Damn, I've *got* to hire another bartender. This week."

He clicked on the cordless and tucked it against his ear. "Yeah, I'm here, Bruce," he said, his voice gravelly. "I'm on my way."

He hung up the phone and glanced back at Jade, torn between duty and fulfilling the awesome need she evoked in him. "I've got to go," he said reluctantly.

Her gaze was smoky with passion, but there was understanding there, too. "Yeah, you do." Pressing her palms against his jaw, she brought him down for another soul-searing kiss. A kiss as erotic as making love. As promising as the emotions blooming between them. She held nothing back, and in that moment Kyle knew she was ready, mind and body, to take the next step in their relationship.

He groaned, in frustration and pleasure, when she finally ended the mind-blowing kiss. Staring at her face, at the stark desire reflected there, a regretful smile tugged at his mouth.

"Hold that thought, tiger."

8

JADE HELD ON TO that tantalizing thought for the rest of the night, wanting Kyle with a restlessness that hummed through her body in a thrilling, provocative sort of way. In a way she knew wouldn't ebb until Kyle satisfied the burgeoning desire he so skillfully roused within her.

After rubbing peach-scented body lotion on her freshly showered skin, she donned a lavender gauze nightie with a ruffled hem that skimmed her calves. As she stared at her reflection in her dresser mirror and traced the lacy bodice that dipped low enough to reveal a swell of cleavage, she found herself wishing Kyle was there, touching her so sensually.

Her need for him had flourished to awesome proportions over the few weeks they'd spent together, grown past friendship to something stronger and more promising. And while at one time she would have panicked at such emotional and physical intimacy with a man, she no longer feared the unknown with Kyle, but welcomed it instead.

When her thoughts strayed to her relationship with Adam, instead of the belly-churning turmoil that usually accompanied such a recollection, Jade only experienced a mellow kind of acceptance for something that had happened in the past.

Kyle was nothing like Adam, and she was so tired of being alone. So weary of solitary nights with only a fantasy lover for companionship. She had no idea how her relationship with Kyle would end. She couldn't predict the future, but she could live for the present. And that meant taking risks. And trusting the instincts that told her Kyle was a good, honest man.

Pulling back the covers on her four-poster bed, she retrieved her sapphire blue journal from her nightstand and settled herself against the mounds of pillows against the headboard. Opening the book to the next blank page, she began writing:

He is the perfect lover in every way. Physically he is a woman's dream come true, a cross between a reckless rebel and a delightful rogue. Emotionally he is tender, caring and kind. No longer is he a fantasy, but a real, flesh-and-blood man. A man who senses my deepest secrets and understands my biggest fears. A man who knows my wildest desires and makes them reality. The bond between us is unspoken, but almost tangible in its strength.

My longing for him is like nothing I've ever experienced. He looks at me and I shiver in anticipation. He touches me and I'm breathless with need. His fleeting caresses and rapacious kisses are no longer enough. I yearn for that deep, physical joining that makes two people one.

Fantasy becomes reality.

I can feel him sliding his powerful, naked body over mine, settling between my parted thighs, then moving deep inside me in a way that is both fierce and tender. His eyes are a brilliant blue as he watches me come undone, his tousled hair as warm as gold. His smile makes me feel like the most beautiful woman on earth.

Kyle.

I'm his, and he is mine. Heart, body and soul...

Heart pounding, body aroused, Jade closed her eyes and hugged her leather-bound journal to her chest. Oh, Lord, she'd done it. Not only had she finally consummated a fantasy, but she'd given her lover a real face and a name: Kyle.

The significance of what she'd done wasn't lost on her. For three years she'd avoided the ultimate act of intimacy with her fantasy lover, choosing instead to keep her entries as safe as real life, by keeping herself emotionally detached and completely in control.

She was still in control, she realized, and ready to move on. Ready to let Kyle into her mind, her body and possibly into her heart. And by doing so, her fantasies would never be the same. The thought was exciting enough to make her quiver.

The cordless phone on her nightstand rang, and she smiled. Even before she answered it, she knew who it was.

Her every fantasy.

Her lover.

Kyle.

She reached for the receiver.

"HELLO?"

The sound of Jade's hushed voice washed over Kyle, the sexy, husky nuances making his tired body come alive. "Did I wake you?"

"No, I couldn't sleep." He heard a rustling sound, a drawer open and close, then she said, "Are you home?"

"Yeah." Moving to his sliding door in his bedroom he opened it and stepped out onto the balcony. Across the courtyard, a light illuminated Jade's bedroom, and although he could see the foot of her bed, he couldn't see her. "I debated whether or not to come by your place, but it's after midnight, and I thought it best if I didn't." If he had, he would have finished what they'd started earlier on his couch, before they'd gotten interrupted.

"I understand. Busy night at the bar?"

Deep, incredulous laughter rumbled in his chest. "It was crazy. Insane. Everybody's talking about the new restaurant and stopping in to find out when the grand opening is. I posted the menu, and it's getting a great response. Only the critics' reviews will tell, though."

"Don't sweat the small stuff, Stephens," she teased. "Another few weeks and The Black Sheep will be swamped."

He smiled at her faith in him. "In another few weeks I'll have enough employees to handle the overflow."

"You're moving up in the world."

There was a sassy smile in her voice that made him grin in return. "Or at least in Santa Monica."

"Everyone needs to start somewhere, and considering what you started with, I think you've done pretty darn good."

It was a heady, overwhelming feeling. Kyle Stephens, responsible, respected business owner. Too bad his family wasn't impressed with what a moral, upstanding citizen he'd become.

Rubbing at the tense muscles along the back of his neck, he resolutely dismissed that line of thought, not wanting old resentments to intrude on his time with Jade. Not tonight.

"So, what are you doing up this late?" he asked.

"Writing a...a letter."

He caught her hesitation, and wondered if she'd

stopped herself before saying "fantasy." He was positive she'd been writing in her journal...and felt a stab of jealousy, which was ridiculous, considering her fantasy lover was nothing more than a figment of her imagination. But dammit, he didn't want to be runner-up to someone who didn't even exist! Not anymore.

He searched the shadows in her bedroom, and guessed she was still sitting on her bed. He needed to see her, if only at a distance. "Are you on a cordless phone?"

"Yes."

"Go out on your balcony."

"I'm hardly dressed for that."

Her sudden bout of modesty was endearing and frustrating. "It's late and dark. Nobody else is out. I want to see you, Jade." He wanted more than that, so much more, but this glimpse of her would have to do for tonight.

"All right," she murmured.

He waited until she came into sight, watching intently as she rounded her big, four-poster bed and headed toward the door. A translucent gown the color of pale lavender swirled around her body, down to her calves. She looked soft and ethereal, like an angel. He was feeling anything but saintly.

Opening the screen door, she stepped out onto the terrace. "Hi," she said, her voice shy.

"Hi, yourself." He braced his forearms on the railing. "I missed you tonight."

A soft sigh drifted through the phone lines. "I missed you, too."

Good God, had anyone besides his daughter ever *really* missed him in his lifetime? He didn't think so. And to think that Jade cared that much was enough to humble him.

His gaze traveled down the length of her, visually outlining the curve of her full breasts tipped with dark centers, the indent of her waist, the flare of her hips and her long, slender legs. He smiled when he saw the gold shimmering at her ankle.

"Do you know," he began, his voice low and hushed, "with the light from your bedroom, I can see your body perfectly silhouetted beneath your gown?"

"Do you like what you see?"

A slow grin curved his mouth. "Very much." He sensed a change in her, that acquiescence he'd so patiently waited for. He planned to take advantage of it. "I like everything about you, Jade. Your smiles, your laughter, your spirit and the sweet, breathless sounds you make when I touch you. It makes me wonder what sounds you'll make when I'm deep inside you."

"Kyle..."

It wasn't a protest. Not really. His name on her lips held an arousing combination of excitement and shivery need. "Close your eyes, Jade. I want to tell you one of my fantasies."

Even from across the moonlit courtyard he could see her body tense. "One of your fantasies?"

There was enough hesitation in her voice to warn him he'd touched on something sensitive. He was feeling reckless enough to push limits. "You inspire fantasies, Jade. Are your eyes closed?"

Another pause, then, "Yes."

"Good. Imagine my mouth on your neck, trailing warm, damp kisses on your skin. My hands on your breasts, caressing you, making your nipples hard and sensitive. Can you feel me?"

"Yes," she whispered.

He watched her shift restlessly on her feet, watched her diaphanous gown shift over her lush curves. His body grew hard, aching, but that was nothing new. He'd been wanting Jade for over seven months now.

He drew a deep, steady breath and continued. "My mouth is on your breast, my tongue curling around your nipple. You taste sweet, Jade, like peaches and cream. I want to taste you everywhere...along your belly, the inside of your thighs and where you're honey sweet and warm. Is your body quivering for me?"

A quiet groan reached him, the sound as erotic as the fantasy he wove. "Yes."

His heart thudded in his chest, and the muscles in his belly pulled taut. "That's exactly how I want you, Jade, but I wouldn't leave you wanting for long. I'd kiss you softly, lingeringly...until you came for me. Then I'd be deep inside you, with your legs wrapped tight around my hips. Me a part of you, and you a part of me. Do you want that, too?"

"Oh, yes." He watched her hand flutter to the neckline of her gown, heard her labored breathing over the phone. "I'm ready, Kyle."

"Ready for what, sweetheart?" he prompted gently.

"To make love with you." Her voice was strong and undeniably confident, clear of any uncertainties or doubts.

A deep, internal shudder ripped through him, primitive and raw and filled with masculine satisfaction. "Do you realize it's taking every ounce of willpower I possess not to be there in ten seconds flat and spend the entire night making love to you?"

"What's stopping you?" she asked, a husky challenge in her tone.

She was a witch...a sassy, sensual witch he was hard-pressed to deny. But deny her he did. "I want to do it right."

"Oh, I don't doubt that you will."

Her double entendre made him chuckle. That she felt comfortable enough to be so playful with him gave him hope for their relationship. "You can count on it, tiger. Have sweet dreams." He disconnected the line and watched her do the same. She lifted a hand to her lips, blew him a sultry kiss from across the courtyard, then slipped back inside her bedroom and out of sight.

Kyle shook his head. He had to be completely nuts to refuse such a tempting invitation. She wanted him, was more than willing to make love with him. And he wanted that so badly his body throbbed with the knowledge. But physical pleasure was no longer his main goal. Somewhere along the way a simple, no-strings-attached affair had evolved into something deeper and more complex.

He wasn't crazy. What he was, he realized in a dazed state of awe, was in love. There was no other explanation for the strange, roller coaster of emotions he experienced around Jade. Or the worthy, invincible way she made him feel. And for the first time in his life he wanted to put someone else's needs above his own selfish desires.

If that wasn't love, he didn't know what was.

Giving himself time to adjust to this newest revelation, he stood out on his balcony, gazing at Jade's condo long after she'd turned out the lights.

A smile touched his mouth. Yes, it was time for them to make love. And he planned to give Jade a fantasy she'd never forget.

"SO WHAT ARE YOUR PLANS for the weekend?"

Jade glanced up at her sister and continued cleaning off her desk. It was Friday afternoon, and while her weekend plans once consisted of spending an occasional evening at Roxy's, the nightclub scene no longer appealed to her.

Now she found she preferred spending her time at The Black Sheep, even if it was just sitting at the bar listening to country tunes and watching the clientele while Kyle worked the lounge.

She gave a noncommittal shrug. "I don't really have any plans."

Mariah strolled deeper into her office. "No hot date with Kyle?"

"'Fraid not." She stuffed a client file into her attaché, just in case she had time to work on it this weekend. It was a depressing thought, but a distinct possibility considering she hadn't seen much of Kyle that week, despite their very seductive and promising conversation out on the terrace the previous Saturday.

"Kyle's been pretty busy at The Black Sheep," she explained to her sister, who'd made herself comfortable in one of the chairs in front of her desk. "The construction of the restaurant is in its final stages, and he's been conducting interviews for chefs and waiters all week." Kyle had even told her he'd offered Bruce the position of managing the restaurant and bar, which the other man had accepted, much to Kyle's relief. He trusted Bruce implicitly.

"How's everything going with the decorating?" Mariah asked.

"Right on schedule." Jade set her attaché on the carpeted floor and tossed a few invoices back into her IN basket to review on Monday. "Kyle decided to shut down the bar all of next week so we can knock everything out at once and keep the liability risk to a minimum. I have a company going in to strip and refinish the floors and bar, and another crew set up to reupholster the booths and bar stools. The window treatments and fixtures are going in, too. By the time the bar is refurbished, the restaurant will be ready to start decorating."

Mariah's eyes sparkled enthusiastically. "I can't wait to see the portfolio on The Black Sheep when it's done."

Jade grinned, pleased with herself and the project. "Will you and Grey come to the grand opening?"

"Are you kidding? We wouldn't miss it. Besides, it'll be the perfect excuse for us old married folk to go out on a date." She winked at Jade, a sly smile lifting her lips. "I'll get Mom and Dad to baby-sit Kayla, maybe even convince them to keep her overnight. Grey's been hinting around that Kayla needs a brother or sister before she's too old to play with them."

Jade laughed, though she experienced a healthy dose of envy for what her sister shared with Grey, for the family Mariah had created with such love and care. As much as she denied needing anyone, and tried to convince herself that her independence was far more important than the confinements of a committed relationship, it was becoming increasingly difficult to ignore the maternal emotions creeping up on her. Since turning thirty, her damned biological clock was starting to tick with disturbing clarity.

She'd known when she'd agreed to an affair with Kyle that he wasn't interested in anything beyond a mutual pleasurable fling. That had been her goal, as well. But somewhere along the way her emotions had gotten tangled up in what should have been a simple and satisfying arrangement between lovers.

"Did you ever find that book you were looking for?"

Jade blinked and lifted her gaze to Mariah. "No." She'd decided she was being paranoid about the journal, especially when she'd started to imagine Kyle's seduction tactics were suspiciously similar to fantasies of the past. "With all the cleaning and shifting of furniture I did before the yard sale, it could be anywhere."

Mariah nodded thoughtfully. "Since it sounds like

you're going to be solo this weekend, what do you say we go shopping together, get our nails done and do lunch?"

"I'm not sure, Riah." The offer was tempting, but if Kyle had a spare moment, she wanted to spend it with him.

A delicate brow rose. "You're actually turning down a day to shop? Boy, you *must* have it bad for Kyle."

She frowned. When had her sister become a mind reader? Not willing to elaborate on emotions she felt so uncertain about, she said, "I'll think about it and let you know tomorrow morning, okay?"

"Sure."

Pam's voice cut through the intercom on Jade's desk. "Jade, there's a man here asking to see you. He says he's here to deliver a private message."

Since Pam had met Kyle before, she knew it wasn't him. And if it wasn't Kyle, then who was this mystery courier? And what kind of message was he attempting to deliver? "I'll be right there."

Smiling, Mariah stood. "Hmm, sounds intriguing."

Jade rounded her desk and headed out of her office with Mariah following close behind. "It's probably just a note from a client."

"Probably." Mariah's tone was dubious.

The older man waiting in the reception area wasn't your normal messenger. He wore a black suit, black gloves and a black bill cap. When she identified herself, he handed over an envelope. Her stomach fluttered when she recognized her name written in Kyle's bold scrawl.

She thanked the man, but he didn't seem inclined to leave. Instead he clasped his hands behind his back and told her he was supposed to wait for a response.

Curious, as was her avid audience of two, she opened the envelope and withdrew the floral-embossed card tucked inside. Mariah leaned close to read the message, but Jade tilted the card away and gave her sister a look that conveyed she wasn't about to share the personal note.

Jade,

The man delivering this message is a hired driver.
There is a limousine waiting outside for you to take you on a special adventure, a fantasy, if you will. Do you trust me? If so, go with the driver, as you are. If not, tell him his services are not required and I'll understand.

Kyle

Jade put the card back in the envelope, trying to still the wild beating of her heart. Her decision was an easy one, driven by her feelings for Kyle.

"Well?" Mariah asked, her exasperation and impatience evident.

Jade glanced at her sister and laughed, feeling carefree and reckless and more than ready for Kyle's adventure. "It looks like my plans for the weekend have just changed."

THE ADVENTURE KYLE SENT her on consisted of a fun and playful scavenger hunt. The first stop the limousine driver made was to a florist, where two dozen dark red roses awaited her, arranged in cellophane so she could enjoy the rich, floral fragrance. The attached card read: *This is only the beginning.*

On the driver went, this time parking the long stretch limo in front of a candy shop. He returned minutes later with a gold foil-wrapped box secured with a wide gold ribbon.

While he headed to their next destination, she opened her newest surprise. As soon as she lifted the lid, her mouth watered at the delectable fragrance teasing her senses. She grinned, then laughed to herself when she realized the contents: Peach wedges dipped in chocolate. She was tempted to sample one, but the enclosed card read: *To share later,* so she waited.

Her journey continued on to P.J.'s Lingerie and Things, a lavish and exclusive boutique. She watched through the tinted window as the driver entered the establishment, then returned with a box tucked beneath his arm. He opened the back door, set it on the seat opposite where she sat, then retrieved a small envelope from the breast pocket of his coat and handed it to her.

As the limousine merged back into traffic, Jade read Kyle's latest offering. The short note was enough to send a prickle of apprehension skittering along her nerves.

Wear this for me tonight.

There was no doubt in her mind the box contained his selection of intimate apparel. She didn't reach for it, too lost in the past, and another man's slow and methodical transformation of her appearance. Just like this note, it all had started so innocently...subtle suggestions that gradually escalated into specific demands that eventually shaped and molded her into a compliant, docile woman.

She chewed on her bottom lip as she stared at Kyle's note, rereading his command. She'd sworn three years ago that she'd never let another man have that kind of control over her, would never let another man dictate her choices.

She looked at each one of his decadent gifts, knowing this last present, like all the rest, was just a part of the special evening Kyle had planned—no other ulterior motives involved. Kyle wasn't trying to change her, would never manipulate her emotions or steal her self-confidence. She'd like to believe she knew him that well. She'd like to believe her judgment hadn't failed her again.

The limousine came to another stop, and Jade resolutely tucked away the doubts and fears that had kept her so isolated and lonely for three years. She wanted this evening with Kyle, and whatever the night might hold.

Her door opened, and the driver smiled down at her. "This is your final destination, Ms. Stevens."

Placing her hand in his gloved one, she stepped from the limo and gazed up at the posh, elite hotel towering in front of her, feeling breathless with anticipation. A bellboy automatically stepped up to the curb and loaded her few items on a cart. The limo driver handed the friendly young man a key and a tip, then another envelope to Jade, instructing her to read it once she was in her room.

"Right this way, miss," the bellboy announced, and led the way through a lobby inlaid with marbled floors. A gorgeous gold-tone fountain dominated the center of the hotel, and a huge, sparkling crystal chandelier hung from the ceiling, casting incandescent prisms all around her. The hotel was exquisite, the furnishings rich and opulent. So was the suite she ended up in. She couldn't help but think how much this wonderful adventure of Kyle's had cost him. A fortune, no doubt.

Once the bellboy unloaded her things and placed her roses on the coffee table, he graced her with a pleasant smile. "Enjoy your stay," he said, then closed the door behind him as he left.

"Wow," Jade murmured, in awe of the extravagance of the suite. She stood in a living room twice the size of her own with a couch, loveseat and huge screen TV—which she guessed wouldn't get much use during their stay. Plush cream carpet covered the floor and complimented the mauve and pale blue accents in the room. There was an adjoining dining area with a table set with fine china, gorgeous cut crystal goblets and gleaming silverware. There was even a small kitchen area with a stocked refrigerator.

There certainly was no need for them to leave any time soon. The amenities were fabulous and extravagant and made Jade feel like a queen. The only thing missing was Kyle.

Remembering the note she held, she opened the envelope and read the enclosed card. *Go into the bedroom and follow the trail of rose petals.*

Intrigued and excited, she opened the double doors just off the living room, revealing a master bedroom with a four-poster Victorian bed covered with a beautiful floral spread and lacy, frilly pillows. An armoire was situated against one wall, along with a matching oval dressing mirror. A chaise longue sat in the far corner. She smiled when she saw the trail of silky red petals sprinkled on the carpet. Breathing in the subtle scent of roses, she followed the path into a sumptuous bathroom.

She gasped, enthralled and delighted by the romantic ambiance someone had so painstakingly created. The sunken tub, large enough for two, was filled with steaming, fragrant water, a froth of bubbles, and topped off with more rose petals. Candles were lit around the tub, soft music played from the speakers built into the ceiling, and a bottle of wine chilled in an ice bucket on the second step leading into the tub. Propped against the fluffy cream towels placed on the rim was yet another brief note. *Relax and enjoy your bath. I'll be with you soon.*

Smiling at that thought, she went back into the living

room and brought the box from the boutique into the bathroom, leaving the contents to be revealed later. Pouring herself a glass of chilled wine, she kicked off her heels and curled her toes into the plush carpet. Leisurely she slipped out of the blouse and skirt she'd worn to work, then stripped off her underthings.

She switched off the vanity lights, leaving the flickering candles as the only source of illumination, then slid into the bath. The warm, silky water, the wine and the music lulled her until her entire body felt boneless. Sighing blissfully, she closed her eyes and sank shoulder-deep into the water.

Her mind drifted, recalling a fantasy she'd written long ago. The setting was similar, the atmosphere drenched with the same provocative sensuality. A steamy, fragrant bath...candles...and strong hands sliding over her slick skin...

Something brushed along the curve of her breast beneath the frothy water. She thought she'd imagined the fleeting caress until that same something glided along her belly. Her eyes flew open on a startled squeak the same time her hand swept through the water, latching on to a wrist that wasn't hers.

Heart lodged into her throat, she stared at the golden-haired rebel who'd become her fantasy lover, in her mind and in reality. He sat on the second step of the tub, his blue eyes filled with heat and sin. And a tenderness that made her ache deep inside. He was shirtless, his chest magnificently bare, his skin warm and inviting looking.

"Close your eyes," he murmured.

He waited for her to comply, his intense gaze never leaving hers. *Go with the fantasy,* her mind urged. With a shiver that stripped her reserve, she did. Releasing his hand, she reclined in the tub and let her lashes drift shut.

The next sensation she experienced was the big bathing sponge she'd seen next to the spigot. The texture was soapy soft and luxurious as he dragged it along her shoulder, then dipped beneath the water, lightly grazing her skin from the peaked tips of her breasts, down her belly and between her thighs that automatically parted for him. He took his time washing her, and arousing her, stroking along sensitive, aching places without fulfilling the promise of his touch. She bit back a moan, feeling feverish and too close to the edge.

Her body hummed and her breathing grew ragged. She was so lost in sensation, so caught up in the fantasy he orchestrated with such unerring accuracy, that it took her a few moments to realize he was no longer touching her. She waited, then slowly opened her eyes and looked around.

Her fantasy lover was gone.

9

JADE STARED AT HER reflection in the bathroom mirror, pleasantly surprised and pleased with Kyle's taste in women's lingerie. Before opening the box from P.J.'s, she'd expected to find a sinfully erotic negligee, a scrap of nothing that left little to one's imagination. Instead she'd discovered something infinitely more delightful.

The apricot-hued chemise Kyle had chosen was an old-fashioned blend of romance, innocence and sensuality, appealing to her softer, feminine side. The delicate stretch lace bodice shaped to her breasts, with a thin ribbon lacing up the center that tied into a dainty bow. The gown itself draped softly along her body to just above the knee, hinting at curves rather than ostensibly clinging to them. The matching bikini panties were made of the same stretch lace, sheer as a sigh, and nothing innocent about them.

Drawing in a deep breath, she met her gaze in the mirror. Gone was the sassy, carefree woman she'd displayed to the outside world. The woman with the green-golden brown eyes staring back at her was the Jade she'd kept hidden from everyone for the past three years. The vulnerable Jade. The Jade who wanted to believe in romance and happily-ever-afters so badly she'd created fantasies for just that reason.

But tonight was no fantasy, but reality in its purest sense.

And she was ready for it.

Before the jittery feeling in her stomach convinced her otherwise, she opened the bathroom door and stepped into the bedroom. More candles had been lit, giving the room a soft, iridescent glow. The bed had been turned down, the mattress sprinkled with more rose blossoms.

A movement from the corner of the room caught her eye. Glancing in that direction, she found Kyle sitting on the chaise longue, long legs stretched out and hands clasped over his belly. Dark, sexy eyes traveled from her face and slowly swept the length of her, making her body flush with a wanting so strong her knees threatened to buckle.

She didn't know what to do. Didn't know what an earthy, sexual man like Kyle expected. Her very limited experience in sex consisted of losing her virginity to a guy she'd been dating in college, a quick awkward romp in the back seat of his Mustang. And then there'd been Adam, who'd expected her to behave the way he thought was appropriate for a lady, in public and in the privacy of his bedroom—accommodating to *his* desires.

And the fantasies she'd written since Adam were just that—her own fictional version of romance and sexual desires. Now that she was facing reality for the first time in years, doubts and uncertainties surfaced. What if she didn't please this man who'd so expertly pleased her? Worse, what if he found her lacking?

"You're nervous," he said perceptively, his voice a rich, low rumble of sound in the shadowed room.

"A little," she admitted, her heart beating heavily beneath her breast. "It's been a long time."

"Yeah, for me, too." His smile was warm and tender. "But you were definitely worth the wait."

So was he, she realized. Confidence restored, she stepped toward him.

"Stop right there," he said, his tone commanding and compelling enough to make her immediately comply.

She waited for him. He didn't move, just sat there on the chaise. His gaze held hers, mesmerizing and disturbingly intense.

"Do you trust me?" he asked.

She remembered the note he'd sent her that had started this provocative adventure of his. "I came here, didn't I?" Her tone was as impatient as she was starting to feel.

"Yes, but what's going to happen tonight is going to change a lot of things between us. And before anything happens, I want to hear that you trust me enough to do anything I ask."

Desire and ingrained apprehension mingled. "I...I do."

"Then untie the bow on the front of your nightgown."

Despite her promise to trust him, the part of her that refused to be dominated or controlled rebelled. She wasn't sure she liked where this game of his was heading. And she certainly wouldn't put up with being ordered around. "Kyle, I don't—"

"Do it," he said, cutting off her protest, "or the fantasy ends."

His use of the word *fantasy* startled her, made everything within her snap to full awareness. "Fantasy?" Her cautious question demanded an explanation.

"Yeah. Mine, yours and soon to be ours," he said mildly, a private, beguiling smile brushing across his mouth. "The latter is solely up to you."

The choice was hers. She could either stop this erotic game of his now, knowing she'd regret her decision later, or she could go with Kyle's fantasy, *their fantasy*, and see where it would lead.

Misgivings and inhibitions fled. She reached for the satin ribbon and tugged. The bow unraveled, the ties loosening as her breasts swelled and her nipples strained against the stretchy lace bodice.

She thought she heard him groan, but couldn't be sure. His gaze was hooded as he watched her. Her eyes drifted lower, where his wide, bare chest expanded with each breath he took. The erection confined beneath the zipper of his jeans gave her a thrilling rush of feminine power she'd never experienced before.

In that moment, she realized she held her own share of control in this seduction. And she decided she was going to use it to drive *him* crazy.

Her mouth curved with a sultry smile of a woman confident in her sensuality. Without waiting for further instructions, she slipped her finger beneath the thin strap of her chemise, eased it over her shoulder and down her arm, then repeated the slow process with the other strap. The stretchy lace molded to her breasts, but she teased the edge with her fingers, gradually dragging it lower, until the lacy material bunched around her ribs and her breasts sprang free, full and aching.

This time Kyle's groan was unmistakable. So was the quiver of excitement blossoming within her.

What had ever made her think this chemise was innocent? At the moment, it was the sexiest, most enticing piece of lingerie she'd ever worn. Daringly, she hooked her thumbs beneath the scrunched lace, inched it down her belly, then shimmied it over her hips. With a final push, the gown slithered down her legs and pooled at her feet. A sudden surge of modesty kept her from removing her panties.

Kyle moved off the chaise and toward her in a lazy, unhurried stroll. He circled around her without touching her, and she began to tremble with a need so great it was all she could do to stand still.

He stopped behind her, and with his hands on her hips, he moved her two steps to the left, until they both came into view of the oval dressing mirror. Another fantasy flashed through her mind, of watching her lover arouse her, but she refused to let it intrude on this wonderful reality.

She stared at their reflection, haloed in a golden glow from the candlelight. Kyle towered over her, his broad frame visible behind her in the mirror. His smoldering gaze met hers, and he smiled as he glided his large hands over the indent of her waist and up to cup her full breasts in his palms. His thumbs grazed over her sensitive nipples, making them peak and tighten. A moan rolled into her tight, aching throat.

"So beautiful," he purred against her neck, his breath a warm caress that sent shivers through her. He slipped his fingers into the sides of her panties, caught the elastic band around his thumb, and whispered in her ear, "Watch."

She was too mesmerized to do otherwise. Her gaze remained riveted on the mirror as Kyle slowly dragged her panties over her hips, then inched them down her thighs, baring her. His warm, damp mouth nuzzled the nape of her neck, then pressed kisses down each vertebra as he slid that scrap of lace lower. By the time his sweet, tormenting lips reached the base of her spine and her panties tangled around her ankles, her entire body thrummed with a wanting greater than anything she'd ever known.

He nipped gently at her buttocks, and shock waves of pleasure rippled through her. When his tongue gently soothed the love bite, she all but melted. Her hands clenched into fists at her sides. She wanted to touch him, feel his strength beneath her fingertips, make his body come alive the same way he was making hers burn.

"Kyle..." It was all she could manage.

"Turn around, Jade." The command was husky and gentle at the same time.

Jade took one last quick look in the mirror, her gaze dropping to just below her bikini line, to the dainty, but permanent reminder of her brief rebellion after Adam. The colorful but delicately etched butterfly was her most private, treasured indulgence, and one she'd never regretted.

But that didn't mean she wasn't the tiniest bit nervous about someone discovering her intimate secret for the first time.

Stepping from her panties, she turned and faced Kyle. He sat back on his heels, his hot gaze devouring every feminine detail of her body. Unable to remain unaffected by his bold perusal, she flushed from head to toe. Never had she felt so vulnerable. So susceptible. Physically and emotionally. She resisted the urge to snatch her chemise back up from the floor and cover herself.

He reached out and touched her, smoothed his splayed hands up her trembling thighs. "Ah, Jade, you're perfect," he murmured, his voice smoky with passion. His thumbs brushed over the brown curls protecting her femininity, slid sinuously into the dampness and heat of her body, and skillfully stroked her with the dewy moisture greeting his touch. "Absolutely perfect."

She moaned. Her head fell back and her body arched toward his questing fingers. Feeling a familiar sensation tingling in every vital, feminine spot, she reached out and grabbed his shoulders for support. When he slicked his thumb, warm and exquisitely wet from her, over her tattoo, her breath whooshed out of her lungs.

"You're full of surprises, tiger, aren't you?" There was a pleased smile in his dark voice. He leaned forward, pressed a hot, openmouthed kiss on her tattoo, and licked away the intimate moisture he'd just rubbed there as if sampling a rare delicacy.

Before she could recover from that shuddering, sensual onslaught, that soft, wicked tongue of his moved impatiently on, tasting her skin, swirling into her belly button, then lapped upward, to her breasts. He suckled her, teased her, tormented her with his mouth, his teeth, his tongue, until she was whimpering, gasping and rubbing against him in a shockingly wanton way. Never, in all her fantasies, could she have imagined such raw hunger, such burning need as she experienced with Kyle.

Gently he grasped the hands digging into the muscles along his shoulders and placed them on his chest. He lifted his head to look at her. The wild beating of his heart beneath her palm, and the tight line of his expression told of his restraint. The glittering heat in his gaze told of his desire for her...the same need that ran thick and molten through her veins.

Slowly he dragged her hands down honed muscles and hot skin. Her fingertips grazed over the light, sexy trail of hair swirling around his navel then disappeared beneath the front waistband of his jeans. He stopped there, removed his guiding hands from her slender wrists, then threaded all ten of his fingers through her hair, tilting her face up to his. "Undress me," he dared in a soft whisper, and lowered his mouth to hers.

It was extremely difficult to accept a challenge, let alone concentrate on it when she felt as if she was drowning—in the slow, silken, heated pleasure of his kiss. Desperate with the need to have him as naked as she, to feel him deep inside her, she fumbled with the top button of his jeans and struggled the zipper over the huge bulge tightening the front of his pants. She nearly cried out in relief when finally, the front placket spread open. Not wasting a second of time, she slid her flattened palms into the waistband of his jeans and boxer shorts, pushed them over his lean hips, slid the soft, faded material over his buttocks and down his hard, toned thighs.

Amazingly, without breaking the lush, seductive kiss, he managed, with a few growls of frustration that reverberated deliciously against her lips, to step from the confining denim and kick it aside.

She wrapped her hand around his shaft, and he shuddered and groaned into her mouth. She stroked the thick length of him in her palm, glanced her thumb over the plum tip, and was rewarded with a drop of moisture that made her realize just how close she *was* to driving him crazy.

It was a heady, exhilarating feeling, and she reveled in it.

Kyle sucked in a ragged breath as Jade continued to tease him to the brink of mindlessness. After weeks of dreaming about making love to her, he wasn't about to have the sizzling sexual buildup end in the palm of her hand. He'd like to think he had more finesse and control than a horny teenager, but that's exactly how she made him feel, like a lust-crazed kid experiencing sex for the first time.

The familiar tightening in his loins warned him how close he was to an explosive orgasm. Grabbing her wrist, he jerked her hand away from his jutting flesh the same moment he broke their lengthy kiss. "Stop," he hissed.

She looked up at him, her eyes wide and startled and brimming with confusion.

He swore mentally, disgusted with himself. Certainly Jade's fantasy lover had never had so little self-control!

He needed to explain, to wipe away the doubt in her expression, and drummed up the patience to do so. "Sweetheart, I want you so badly that if you don't stop touching me the way you are it's going to be over before it even starts. Unfortunately, Charlie has a mind of his own, and when you touch him, the only thing he can think of is how soft and warm your hand is, and how much better it would feel to be deep inside you.... The thought is powerful enough to make him think he *is* deep inside you."

When his meaning caught on, strangled laughter caught in her throat.

"It's the truth," he stated, feigning indignation and biding time to allow his ardor to cool before they continued. Framing her face with his hands and staring deep into her eyes, he guided her back toward the bed.

"This first time it's gonna be slow and easy." His lips plucked at hers, drawing a soft sigh from her. He felt her soften, relax, and thought of the endless hours of pleasure that awaited them. "And later, it can be as fast and wild as you want it to be. We've got all night long, tiger...to make love, fulfill fantasies and do all the things to each other we've been wanting to do for months. That *I've* been wanting to do to *you* for months."

"Yes," she said as he pressed her down on the mattress. Her heated skin slid across the soft petals sprinkled over the sheet, releasing a lush, intoxicating fragrance of roses and aroused female flesh that went straight to his head. "Oh, yes."

He lifted a brow as he knelt on the bed by her feet. The intensity of the moment had passed, but he liked this playful side of making love, too. "So, are you admitting there's been a few things you've been wanting to do to me?" He picked up her right foot, pressed a kiss to the sensitive arch, then bit gently into the pad of flesh just beneath her toes.

She gasped, and from his vantage point he watched the muscles in her belly contract, could see her nipples peak as she arched her back sinuously. "Maybe one or two," she all but purred.

"You can have your way with me later." Smiling, he traced the gold anklet adorning her leg—the only thing she wore besides the rosy-hued flush painting her body. "Right now, I'm gonna show you what I've fantasized about doing to you."

Skimming his hands up both her calves, he gently urged her legs apart and moved in between. Then, starting with her right leg, he pressed a damp kiss to the inside of her knee and leisurely nibbled and licked his way up the inside of her thigh. He gave the same treatment to her other leg. By the time he reached his ultimate destination, her body was taut and trembling, her breathing ragged.

"Kyle..." Her quivering voice held a wealth of vulnerability and uncertainties.

"Shh, sweetheart, let me," he murmured. Splaying his hands on the inside of her slender thighs, he pressed his mouth against the heat between her legs, grazed his tongue along the satin-soft feminine folds of her body, wanting her to trust him in every elemental way.

And, incredibly, she did. He felt it in the gradual unfurling of tension in her limbs, tasted it in the sweet wonder of her body, heard it in the sexy, breathless sounds she made. And, ultimately, he experienced it in her unequivocal surrender as he coaxed her to a slow, escalating climax, then sent her soaring over the edge.

She cried out and clutched a fistful of sheet and rose petals as her body writhed with the force of her release.

Once her orgasm ebbed, once she could breathe without gasping, she tangled her fingers in his hair and tugged.

He looked up over her beautifully sprawled, satiated body, meeting eyes fever bright with desire. He continued to caress that ultrasensitive nub of flesh with his thumb, slid a finger deep enough to make her breath catch, and knew it would be so easy to make her come again.

"Tell me what you want, Jade." The decision would be hers. He'd spend the night giving her every physical pleasure she could wish for short of the actual act of making love if that's what she wanted.

"You," she said softly. "I want you...I *need* you, inside me."

A giant shudder reverberated through Kyle. Even in his passion-induced state, the significance of what she was offering, what she was asking for, didn't elude him. Physically, she was giving him her body; emotionally, she was bestowing him with a gift more precious than anything anyone had ever given him before. Complete, unconditional trust. Honest faith. Possibly even love. And damn selfish as it seemed, he wanted everything she was willing to give. Which was everything missing from his life.

He reached for the protection he'd left on the nightstand earlier, but before he could sheath himself, her fingers curled around his wrist, stopping him.

She ran her tongue across her bottom lip. "I went on the Pill after we, umm...agreed to..."

Grinning at her shyness, he lowered his hard, aroused body over hers, threading his fingers through her hair. "I understand, and I'm thoroughly grateful. There's nothing more I'd like than to have nothing between us."

"Me, too." Sighing blissfully, she closed her eyes, dragging her hands down the slope of his back. Automatically, openly, she wrapped her legs around his hips, cradling him close. His erection slipped against soft, damp flesh, unerringly found that place where two became one, and although every molecule within him screamed to thrust hard and deep, he held back.

Jade's lashes lifted, a beguiling smile curling her mouth. "Has it been so long you've forgotten what to do?"

He laughed and started to say something about her sassy mouth, but he got distracted by a sudden discovery. "Hazel," he murmured, awed by his discovery.

She frowned up at him.

"Your eyes," he said, wondering why he hadn't noticed earlier. Probably because he was so used to her hiding behind her colored contact lenses. "They're hazel."

"Yeah, they are," she said shyly.

He smoothed his thumb along her jaw, guessing how difficult it had been for her to bare so much to him, and wondered what it meant in terms of her feelings for him. "They're beautiful, Jade. Green and gold with just a hint of brown at the centers."

Color rose in her cheeks at his compliment, which was endearing considering the other things he'd done to her tonight which hadn't embarrassed her. "They're very ordinary."

"There is nothing ordinary about you." Done talking, he kissed her. A long, wet, passionate kiss that stoked the banked fires within them, until Jade was moving restlessly beneath him, her legs urging him downward, her hands frantically urging his hips forward.

He pushed inside her, stretching her, groaning as her silky heat enveloped him until he was fully embedded inside her body. He was enraptured by the way she complemented him so perfectly. Moved by the fragile, emotional bond linking them in a far more meaningful way than a simple, casual affair.

There was nothing casual about the intense feelings this woman evoked in him. Nothing simple about wanting her in his life when he'd avoided commitment for all his adult years.

She gasped sharply as he began to move, her back arching toward him as he retreated, then returned, surging deep. He softened their kisses, murmured encouragements and darker suggestions, reached between their damp bodies and stroked her where they joined.

Her pleasure became his own. As he followed her into that dark, erotic abyss, he knew what it was like to need someone with every fiber of his being. Knew what it was to want to hold on and never let go. To feel so much, and still need more.

He felt it with Jade.

"OPEN UP AND SAY AHH," Kyle cajoled.

Jade's brows rose. "You don't expect me to take *all* of that in my mouth, do you?"

"Naw," he drawled, smiling wickedly. "Just a little at a time."

Kneeling on the mattress in front of where he stood by the side of the bed, she regarded the tempting offering he held in his hand, while he contemplated just how tousled and incredibly bewitching she looked. After making love she'd donned the chemise he'd bought her; reluctantly, he'd granted her that small measure of modesty for now, though he did notice that she hadn't bothered with the panties. The ribbons on the bodice were still untied, and a thin strap had fallen down one shoulder, giving him a titillating glimpse of her breasts and the way her nipples thrust against the stretchy lace.

Her sexy, kittenish pose reminded him of a page straight out of a centerfold magazine. She looked like every man's carnal fantasy come to life, innocence blended with the hint of sin sparkling in those soft green-gold eyes of hers.

Tilting her head, she slid her tongue provocatively along her bottom lip. "Can I lick the chocolate off?"

His chuckle rolled into a masculine groan. "Tiger, you can do anything you like...and as much as I might enjoy watching that, it's much better if you just try it the way it is." He rubbed the smooth, chocolate-covered tip against her pink lips, still swollen from all the lusty kisses they'd shared earlier. "I was assured this is quite a delicacy."

"Well, I suppose I can open myself to a new experience." She parted her lips, and Kyle slowly, teasingly, slipped the candied wedge of peach into her mouth. Closing her eyes, she bit down. A groan of pure pleasure rolled into her throat as she savored the exotic flavor filling her mouth.

Kyle watched a delightful smile curve her lips, saw the ecstasy chasing across her features, and resisted the urge to pull her to him for a hot, peach-sweet kiss. He knew it would inevitably lead to him dragging her beneath him, nudging her thighs apart, and burying himself so deep inside her warmth and softness there would be no distinguishing where one ended and the other began.

The image caused his masculine parts to stir beneath the front of his boxer shorts. Soon, he thought, enjoying this simple moment of pleasure with Jade far too much for it to end just yet.

He rubbed the sticky-sweet peach along her lips. "More?"

Her lashes lifted slumberously. "Mmm. All of it."

Continuing with their playful innuendo, he feigned shock. "Are you sure you can handle it *all* at once?"

Grasping his wrist, she brought the candied fruit to her lips. "Let's try it and see."

Not only did she eat the peach in one very sensual bite, she licked the melted chocolate from his fingers. She gave the task more attention than it warranted, yet stopped way too soon for his liking.

"That tasted...incredible." She smiled up at him, like a contented feline who'd indulged in a bowl of rich cream. "You do wonderful things with peaches."

He could think of at least a dozen other things he'd like to do with those peaches, to *her*...erotic, decadent games beyond her wildest fantasies. But kept them tucked away for another time.

He reached for the glass of chilled wine he'd put on the nightstand, next to the box of chocolate-covered peaches. "I aim to please," he said, tipping the glass to her lips.

She swallowed a drink, then let her gaze roam appreciatively down his body. "Oh, you do." Her voice was breathless.

He couldn't help but feel a surge of male satisfaction. There was something about this woman that made him *want* to please her.

Settling himself on the bed next to her, and bringing the box of sweets and glass of wine with him, he propped himself up on his elbow.

"This adventure of yours was quite a surprise," Jade said in between him feeding her bites of peaches and sips of wine. She crossed her legs, making herself more comfortable. "I've never felt so special. Thank you."

He smiled. "You deserve to be spoiled, Jade. And I like doing it for you."

She slanted him a look tinged with disbelief. "I never would have pegged you for a romantic."

Before Jade, he hadn't given much thought to indulging the women he'd dated. Had never let any of them close enough for his emotions to get tangled up in the relationship. "There's a first time for everything." Even love, he thought, growing used to the idea of giving Jade a part of himself he'd thought he was incapable of giving. "Besides, you've got a couple of surprises up your sleeve, too. Or should I say, hidden away in your panties."

A blush stole across her cheeks, and she absently smoothed the hem of her chemise over her thighs. "I take it you're referring to my tattoo."

"Ummm...among a few other treasures hidden in your panties," he said wickedly. Feminine wonders he'd thoroughly enjoyed. Definitely unexpected, though, had been her tattoo. "What made you do it, Jade?"

She shrugged. "Just a crazy, wild impulse."

Her explanation seemed too simple. Too easy. "Something must have spurred that impulse. Or someone," he added, suspecting the latter.

She looked away, pretending interest in a watercolor painting on the wall. He wasn't fooled by her evasion. Unwilling to let her avoid this very important discussion, he gently grasped her chin and turned her face to his again. He saw the faintest hint of pain in her eyes, could see her reluctance to drag the past out in the open.

"Tell me, Jade," he urged, experiencing a swell of tenderness that came straight from the heart. "I'm not here to judge you, but I need to know what happened in your previous relationship that has made you so, well... distrusting of men."

She didn't deny his claim. But she didn't venture to elaborate, either.

He sighed, skimming his thumb down the slope of her tense jaw. He'd pursued this very stubborn woman for six months, unexpectedly fallen in love with her in less than two. There was no way he was going to let something so obviously important to their future fall by the wayside.

"You've trusted me with everything else tonight," he went on, attempting a more ruthless, straightforward approach. "I'd like to think you can trust me with your past."

Jade stared at the man who'd come to mean so much to her in such a short span of time. A man who'd tapped into her deepest secrets and desires and restored her confidence as a woman. A man who'd given her so much and asked so little in return.

Needing to relax the knot in her belly, she reached for the glass of wine he held and drained what little was left of the pale gold drink. Liquid courage, she thought with inner mockery as she set the empty glass on the night-stand behind her, then refocused her gaze on anything but Kyle.

"I met Adam Beckman at a cocktail party hosted by a client of mine who owned a finance firm," she began, easily recalling that fateful night. "Adam worked for him. He was quite charming, and I have to admit that flattery got him everywhere." She smiled wanly. "We started dating, and things got serious between us real fast. Before I knew it, I was totally wrapped up in Adam, willing to do anything to please him or to be with him."

She smoothed her damp palms down the cotton covering her thighs, while her heart thudded in her chest. Other than her sister and parents, no one knew how devastating and emotionally destructive her relationship with Adam had been.

She lifted her gaze to Kyle, not sure what she expected

to find. He was quiet, but watchful and tremendously patient. His silent strength gave her the fortitude to go on.

"After a couple of months of dating, Adam started making mild suggestions to change my appearance...like my hair. It was waist-length and thick, and while I liked to wear it down, he preferred it up, though he insisted I not cut it." She found herself touching the wispy hair at the nape of her neck, not regretting the day she'd sheared off the length shortly after her breakup with Adam. That bit of defiance had felt glorious.

"He didn't like makeup, so I started wearing very little, and pale colors at that. Next came my clothes. Adam insisted if I was going to be the girlfriend of a high-powered executive, I needed to look the part." *Not like some trussed-up Barbie doll*, she remembered him saying. "We went shopping for a new wardrobe and Adam chose conservative suits and dresses in dark, drab colors." Looking back, she realized Adam's ploy...to downplay her appearance so he'd upstage her in his fancy, expensive designer clothes. And he had. She later learned he was a man who needed to feel superior, even at the expense of others.

Finding a rose petal in the folds of the sheet, she rubbed the silky-soft blossom between her fingers and spared another glance at Kyle. He said nothing, but the tight line of his jaw spoke volumes. He didn't like what he was hearing. She supposed that made them even, because she hated relaying the awful experience.

"My appearance wasn't all he altered," she said quietly, her voice hushed in the too-quiet bedroom. "Adam was controlling and dominating and had certain ideas of what I should be and how I should act. In public and in private. He even started keeping track of my whereabouts, where I went and who I saw. And I fell right into his trap, letting him influence me to the point that I was no longer the person I'd been before him, but a compliant, docile woman he'd shaped and molded to his warped expectations." It had happened so quickly. Too easily. Frighteningly so. "I was so caught up in our relationship, I couldn't see just how destructive Adam's manipulation was."

Needing space, she slid from the bed and walked over to the floor-to-ceiling window in the room. Kyle had opened the drapes earlier, and from sixteen stories up, they had a fabulous view overlooking the city. The twinkling lights with a backdrop of black velvet soothed the upheaval of emotions within her.

"What happened, Jade?" Kyle asked, his voice strong and steady from behind her.

She shivered and wrapped her arms around her middle, chilled by the memories leaping to life in her mind. The worst was yet to be told, but having already come this far, and trusting Kyle more than she thought possible, she shut out the pain and focused on purging herself of the past.

"My sister and parents expressed their concern over the erratic changes in my behavior and appearance," she said, not daring to look at Kyle for fear of losing her confidence to go on. "A part of me—the part that was in love with Adam—resented their interference and denied the truth. I was determined to prove my family wrong about Adam."

The silence in the room was absolute. He was waiting for her to go on, and she was dreading what lay ahead...reliving the singularly worst night of her life. Her stomach churned, and the pressure in her chest increased to an unbearable tension.

She pushed the turmoil aside. "Adam received a promotion at work, and I threw him a surprise party inviting our friends and family. I wanted to look my best, and I also wanted to show my family that Adam wasn't as bad as they were making him out to be. So I went and had my makeup done, then my hair styled, leaving it down so it fell to nearly my waist in soft waves. I bought a new dress, an ankle-length sheath that was sexy in a very subtle way, though it had a slit that showed more leg than any of the other outfits Adam chose for me."

She touched a hand to the cool windowpane, a faint smile touching her lips. "I remember looking in the mirror, thinking that for the first time since dating Adam I felt pretty, feminine and desirable. My last thought was that I hoped the way I looked pleased him."

She drew in a ragged breath, and let the rest of the story rush out before she could stop it. "But when he walked into the party and saw me talking to a male colleague of his, all dressed up and looking as my sister put it 'like a knockout,' he turned absolutely livid." She shuddered when she recalled how his eyes had flashed with cold fury, how he'd advanced on her with a look of utter contempt, how his voice had dripped pure disgust. "In front of my family and friends, he informed me that he wouldn't be seen with a woman who dressed and acted like a hooker, then left the party being held in his honor."

"Bastard," Kyle muttered from behind her.

"I was completely mortified and humiliated," she said with a choked little laugh, not so surprised to feel the hot sting of tears prick her eyes. She'd been holding them back for three years now. "I just wanted to die of embarrassment."

She heard the creak of the mattress as Kyle got off the bed, saw his reflection in the window as he approached from behind. Felt her taut body sag in relief as he slipped his arms around her waist and pulled her flush against his chest, his belly, his thighs, surrounding her in a wonderful heat that chased away the lingering coldness inside her.

"Ahh, sweetheart," he breathed, his lips pressing gently against her neck. "I'm so sorry."

She closed her eyes, absorbing his warmth and caring while trying to hang on to her composure. "At first, I was devastated," she admitted, needing to finish what they'd started. "But my sister and parents helped me through that crisis. Without Adam's daily influence I realized just how much control he had over me. And it was then I swore I'd never let any man close enough to manipulate me that way again."

Kyle linked their fingers together in front of her, keeping her close, trying to ease the trembling still shimmering through her body. Now he understood her reluctance to get involved with him or any man. And more than ever, her fantasies made sense. With an imaginary lover she was safe to express her wants and needs, without the threat of being controlled, because she was the one to dictate the level of intimacy.

"So, after Adam you rebelled." Like the delightful butterfly of her tattoo, she'd emerged from her cocoon.

"Yeah, I did." She leaned her head against his shoulder. "I went out and bought new clothes in bright colors, cut my hair and even started wearing colored contact lenses to match my outfits. It was my way of coping with what had happened. And to prove just how independent I was, one day I decided to get a tattoo. Something that no one could ever take away from me."

He smiled, understanding her rebellion all too well. He'd coped with his own childhood and his father's disregard with wild, shocking acts of defiance himself.

Feeling as though they'd made tremendous progress

this evening, he turned her in his arms. His eyes found hers, locking tight. "I happen to love your butterfly...but I don't think I like the idea of anyone else seeing it."

She lifted a brow, and he was glad to see the haunting shadows gone from her gaze. "Other than the artist, you're the first person who's seen it. And certainly the first to *touch* it."

He couldn't help himself, his chest puffed out arrogantly. "And I prefer that no one else does."

Too late, he realized just how possessive he sounded...how *dominating*. The way she visibly bristled confirmed it.

"Tiger," he said gently, brushing his knuckles down her cheek. "This isn't a control issue. You've got to believe I'll always respect your independence, and I'd never try to dictate your life." The emotions he'd been holding back welled inside him, demanding release. "But there's something you need to know."

Her brows furrowed above eyes shaded with wariness. "Yes?"

"I'm falling in love with you, Jade." Surprisingly the words he'd never spoken to another woman came much easier than he'd expected. "Never mind falling. Hell, I *am* in love with you."

She gasped in shock, her jaw falling slack.

It wasn't the reaction he'd hoped for, but then he'd had more time to get used to the idea of being in love than the handful of seconds he'd just given Jade. But he'd bet The Black Sheep she felt the same way—she just didn't realize it yet. "I know we agreed to a no-strings-attached affair..." And he'd thought that would be enough. "But somewhere along the way I fell in love with you."

"Oh, Kyle." Jade reached up and lightly touched her fingers to his cheek, shaken to the very core by his declaration, which she found both sweet and terrifying. "I care for you a great deal, but..." *I'm so scared of giving someone that part of myself again. So scared of letting emotions overwhelm my better judgment.*

But she feared she already had.

A tremulous smile touched her lips. "Give me a little time, okay?"

"As much as you want." Grasping her hand, he pressed a kiss in her palm, his eyes glimmering with renewed warmth. "As much as you need. And while you're thinking about it, why don't we enjoy the time we have together? I want you again, Jade. I don't think I'll ever get enough of you."

And she him. "Yes," she whispered. Heated desire coiled through her. The anticipation of his touch, his possession, made her breathless.

In one smooth motion he pushed his shorts down his legs and kicked them off, then pinned her against the wall with his hot, fully aroused body. She moaned as his mouth dropped over hers, his tongue delving deep while his hands slipped beneath the hem of her chemise and skimmed up the back of her thighs to her buttocks. He lifted her, bracing her, the tip of his erection teasing her damp female flesh. She looped her arms around his neck and curled her legs tight about his hips, needing him in a way that went far beyond the physical.

This time, he took her fast and hard, pulling her hips down to meet his hammering upward thrusts...over and over until she was gasping into the crushing force of his mouth and clinging to him, her fingers wrapped tight in his hair. His passionate assault was wild and relentless. Splaying his hands low on her back, he arched her more fully onto him and ground his body full force against hers, creating an exquisite friction that made her tremble.

The stormy tempest broke on a wave of pleasure so intense she wrenched her mouth away and cried out his name. And as she came with a glorious, shuddering climax that beckoned his release, her heart admitted what her mind wasn't yet prepared to accept.

She'd fallen in love with him, too.

10

ONCE THE LAST CUSTOMER of the evening had departed, Kyle locked the oak door inlaid with beveled glass. Then he clicked off the lit-up sign in the front window that said, "The Black Sheep Bar and Restaurant" in a classy, scrolled design. The custom-ordered sign had been a surprise from Jade a few days ago. When he'd protested against such an expensive gift, she'd linked her arms around his neck and teasingly told him she could think of plenty of ways for him to repay her. Then she'd pulled his mouth down to hers for a shockingly brazen kiss that had instantly aroused him.

Not that it took much for him to want her. A look. A touch. The smell of peaches...

They'd ended up on the leather couch in his newly decorated office, so hungry and impatient for one another it was all he could do to shove her skirt up her thighs and strip off her panties. Freeing his straining erection had been a frustrating task; his fingers kept colliding with Jade's eager attempts to help. But that first powerful thrust home had felt so incredibly good and right. Then the wildfire of sensation had spread through him to her, spinning them both out of control.

They'd had many incidents just like that over the past month, making love with an impatient, crazy urgency beyond anything he'd ever experienced. Yet there had been many tender moments, too, when they'd spent hours losing themselves in endless pleasure and new, erotic discoveries that made the fantasies in Jade's journal pale in comparison.

Day by day, hour by hour, he fell deeper in love with her, and knew he wanted things with this woman he'd never dared dream of. Bonds and commitments that had eluded him his entire life.

And the secret he'd kept from her began to prey on his conscience.

The light touch of a hand on his arm pulled him back to the present. Turning, he caught Jade in his embrace. She went willingly, smiling up at him, her eyes bright with the same sense of satisfaction flowing through his veins.

"Didn't I tell you the grand opening would be a success?" she asked, a bit of sass in her tone.

"No less than a hundred times," he admitted, giving credit where it was due. She'd been reassuring him for the past week. He'd been convinced that he'd overburdened himself financially and that the establishment would flounder then sink, like so many businesses did these days, leaving him with a huge debt he'd never recover from. And then his family would have proof that he was just as reckless and irresponsible as they believed.

"Then maybe you ought to listen to me." She twined her arms around his neck, causing his body to acknowledge the fact that she was braless beneath the sexy halter-style minidress she wore. "I know my business, Kyle, and you know yours. Together we make a great team."

In more than just business, he thought, giving in to the urge to smooth his hand over the silky skin of her back and press her closer.

"Besides, how can the new Black Sheep *not* be a success?" Her fingers tangled into the strands of hair falling over the collar of his shirt, and she subtly arched against him. "Just take a look at the place."

Despite the fog of desire quickly stealing coherent thought, he glanced around them. The atmosphere was exactly what he'd envisioned—understated sophistication. Classy, yet warm and welcoming. The hardwood floors and walls gleamed, as did the refinished bar. All the booths and stools had been reupholstered, and the windows were now framed in valances that matched the ones in the restaurant. A deejay booth dominated a section of the lounge; earlier in the evening, the parquet dance floor had been packed as his new deejay played country-western tunes and encouraged the customers to party and have a good time.

And they had, to the point that when the bartender called for last rounds the revelers had been clearly, and vocally, disappointed. Jade had told him it was a sure sign that they would return, and probably bring their friends with them.

As he watched his employees clean up for the evening, he admitted he was even pleased with the uniforms, which he and his manager, Bruce, wore as well. The outfits were polished and crisp, yet casual enough to be comfortable.

"And judging by the two-hour wait to get into the restaurant and the positive comments I heard from everyone, I think The Black Sheep is going to blow Roxy's right out of the water." She skimmed her flattened palms over his shoulders and down the front of his shirt, then gave his tie a gentle, teasing tug. "Even my father was impressed with the place."

His gaze fell to her mouth, so ripe and lush, just inches from his. His pulse quickened. His blood heated. With effort, he remembered the employees still present.

"It was nice of him and your mother to come," he said, meaning it. Considering his own family didn't even acknowledge his profession as respectable, he appreciated the unequivocal support of Jade's family. "And Grey and Mariah, too."

"I think they all like you."

He wiggled his brows and effortlessly eased her into a dark, intimate corner near the door. Slipping a hand down to her bottom and giving it a provocative squeeze, he lowered his mouth close to hers. "What's not to like?" he murmured.

Her light, husky laughter wrapped around him, as did the warm scent of peaches drifting from her skin. "I haven't discovered that flaw yet. It seems that you, Kyle Stephens, are too good to be true."

He'd meant to kiss her, good and long and deep, but the euphoria he'd been feeling moments ago waned with her adulation. Oh, he had flaws, the one weighing heaviest on his mind being deception about the journal. And it grew heavier every day. He was hardly the sterling white knight she was making him out to be.

Her fingers followed the line of his suspenders to the waistband of his slacks. "You know, there's something incredibly sexy about you in a uniform," she whispered in his ear. "You see, I've had this fantasy—"

He groaned and placed his fingers over her lips, knowing *exactly* what that fantasy was, and precisely how it ended—with the taste of Jade on her lover's lips, and her body glistening and quivering with pleasure. That was a fantasy he'd gladly fulfill. Later.

He drew in a steadying breath that did little to ease the desire spiraling deep in his belly. The only thing that had the ability to satisfy that particular craving was sliding deep inside of Jade and hearing her sweet, breathless cries of abandon as her body contracted around his. Her passion, and his hunger for her, were limitless.

"Hold that thought, tiger," he said, dragging his thumb across her bottom lip. "I've got at least another hour to close down the place. And if you don't leave, I'm never going to get out of here, and my employees are going to be shocked by their boss's sexual exploits."

Minutes later they stood next to the driver's side of Jade's Miata. He opened the door for her, but she didn't get inside the car.

She looked up at him, a tremulous, almost nervous smile on her lips. "I know it's late, but how do you feel about coming by my place when you're through here and we can have our own private celebration? I've got a surprise for you."

Instinctively he knew she wasn't talking about a tangible kind of gift. Beneath the street lamp, her hazel eyes shimmered with an emotion he'd only seen glimpses of since he'd told her he was in love with her. And even though he hadn't pushed her to return the sentiment, he knew her feelings for him were just as strong. The soft way he caught her looking at him, the unabashed pleasure that lit her expression when they saw each other after a long day spent apart, and most telling, the way she gave herself so freely to him when they made love, told him more than the words he was waiting for.

And knowing she was falling in love with him made him feel like the richest man on earth, and as guilty as hell for using the journal of fantasies to seduce her.

"Well?" she prompted, a wealth of uncertainties in her voice.

He tucked a wispy cinnamon strand of hair behind her ear, and suddenly knew what he needed to do. "Sweetheart, I'd be out of my mind to refuse such an offer."

This time, her smile was beatific. "I'll be waiting," she promised, then slipped into her sports car.

Kyle pushed his hands into the front pockets of his trousers, watching as she pulled out of the parking lot and drove away. Once her taillights were no longer in sight, he stared at the entrance to The Black Sheep, floating on the natural high that came with achieving recognition for all his hard work and efforts. He'd finally made it on his own. The pride that filled him was awesome, like nothing he'd ever experienced.

As a young boy he'd yearned for approval from a father whom he could never please, sought acceptance from a brother who saw him as competition for their father's affection.

Those early years had shaped him into a rebellious teen, driven by a bitterness and anger that ran deep. Irresponsible, his father had branded him, yet it had been his father's lack of support that had pushed him to such extremes.

It had been the marines that had disciplined him and given his life a new direction, saving him from drifting to the wrong side of the law. The service had given him the responsibility he'd been lacking, made him more respectful and accepting of the way things were.

Yet he still felt the emotional weight of past regrets, especially when he thought about his relationship with Christy, which he wished could be so much more than it was. It was those regrets that made him realize he didn't want to risk losing what he shared with Jade...and the bright promise of a future with her.

He'd always found it easier to be a loner than let anyone close. He'd always believed he didn't deserve the kind of love he'd longed for as a boy. As a grown man, he'd reconciled himself to being a bachelor.

That had been before Jade brought light where there had been only darkness. That was before he knew the depth of his need. Now he knew the richness of love. And he was selfish enough to want to wallow in it for the rest of his life.

The muscles in his belly clenched with apprehension for what lay ahead. He'd asked for Jade's trust, and despite being badly burned in the past, she'd given it to him. If he expected her to ultimately trust him with her heart, with her love, then there was no room for secrets or lies between them.

It was time to give back the journal.

SLIPPING A SILKY ROBE over the short, sexy black negligee she'd donned for Kyle to discover later, Jade padded across her bedroom and opened the drapes and sliding door to let cool night air flow through the room. Across the courtyard, Kyle's condo was dark. She intended for it to remain so for the rest of the night. After tonight's seduction, she planned to wake up in the morning in his arms.

The wait for him was excruciating, made longer by her nervousness. It had taken her three years to open up and trust a man again, but then Kyle was no ordinary man. He was sexy and outrageously straightforward, and while his bold approach and determination had once unsettled her, it now excited her. He was kind, honest and extremely patient, considering most men would have given up on her long ago. It was as though they were connected somehow, on a level so intimate he could sense her fears and vulnerabilities, and some of her deepest secrets and desires, too.

It was inevitable that she fall in love with him. He'd become her fantasy man, in every way. Except Kyle was flesh and blood...and he loved her, an emotion her fantasy lover was incapable of. An emotion she longed to give, as well as receive.

Growing restless, she turned from the open door and roamed around her room, waiting to hear Kyle's knock. Attempting to relax, she sat on the edge of her bed, closed her eyes, and imagined the night ahead as one of her fantasies. She wanted to be everything Kyle could ever want in a woman and in a lover. She wanted to show him, as well as tell him, what was in her heart.

A rustling sound from outside her balcony startled her. Her eyes flew open and she watched, transfixed, as a dark figure pulled himself up along the wrought-iron railing, then effortlessly leapt over it onto the terrace....

He appeared from the shadows of the balcony, the silvery cast of moonlight silhouetting his tall, lean build.... The old fantasy played through her mind, and she blinked twice to make sure she wasn't imagining things. Then the figure started forward, reaching for the screen door and sliding it open.

Good God, this was no illusion or fantasy but an intruder! With a scream lodged in her throat, she turned and scrambled across the bed, grabbing for the cordless phone to call for help as she tumbled off the other end of the mattress. She gained her footing and headed for the bedroom door.

"Jade, it's me, Kyle," a familiar voice said urgently.

She whirled around, adrenaline pumping through her veins. With the dim light from the nightstand she could see that it was Kyle, though there were enough similarities, in coloring and build, it could have been her fantasy lover, too. Standing there, he seemed so imposing. So sexy. And incredibly real. He still wore his shirt, slacks and suspenders, and he was carrying a beige canvas knapsack.

"Dammit, Kyle, you scared me to death sneaking in that way!" She replaced the phone in the unit, still feeling a little shaken.

"You didn't seem frightened," he said, his voice deep and mesmerizing. "Not at first. You looked as though you were expecting someone to come that way. Were you?"

The accuracy of his observation unnerved her. How could he have known? "That's ridiculous."

"Were you waiting for me?" He stepped more fully into the light, allowing her to see the purposeful gleam in his eyes. "Thinking of me?"

She shook off her unease, dismissing the coincidences between fantasy and reality. Determined to remain in control of tonight's celebration, she rounded the bed and slowly approached him. "Yes, I was waiting for you, thinking of you."

"And what were you thinking?" he asked huskily.

"How much I want you." She untied the sash on her robe, gave her shoulders a slight shrug, and let the slippery material slide down her arms and flutter to the floor. "How much I need you."

Kyle's mouth went dry as he stared at the sheer black negligee she wore, unable to overlook the fact that she wore no panties. The sight was erotic enough to distract him from his original purpose.

Reaching him, she drew a finger up his arm and around his neck, slowly circling him. From behind, she murmured into his ear, "Do you want me?"

A giant shudder of need wracked his body. He'd always been the aggressor, but tonight she radiated a sexy confidence he was hard-pressed to discourage. Her shameless approach turned him on, made him anticipate what was to come. "There isn't a minute that goes by that I don't."

She stood in front of him, a soft, provocative smile on her lips as she began unknotting his tie, then slid it from his collar and dropped it carelessly on the floor. Then she pushed his suspenders down his arms and began working on the buttons on his shirt. He was so mesmerized by her feminine prowess, it was all he could do to keep breathing steadily.

She pulled the tail ends from his slacks, then smoothed her cool, flattened palms down his chest, his taut belly, to the black leather belt cinching his waist. Though her gaze held his, she worked the buckle quickly and efficiently. "Remember that surprise I have for you?"

"Yeah." His voice was rough with arousal, rich with need.

Her hazel eyes filled with an emotion so intense and brilliant his heart gave a distinct thump in his chest. "I love you, Kyle Stephens," she said. "More than I believed possible."

He groaned at her sweet, guileless declaration, and the ease in which she pushed his slacks and boxers over his hips and down his legs. Before he had time to assimilate her intent, her hand wrapped around his erection, warm and snug and coaxing.

A hiss of breath escaped him, and he squeezed his eyes shut. His fingers tightened around the leather straps of the knapsack he still held in his hand, forcing him to remember his honorable intentions for this evening. No easy feat considering his body had a different agenda than his head. "Jade...we need to talk."

"Later," she said, just as her hot, wet mouth glanced off his hip, his thigh... Then her tongue curled around him, silky soft and shockingly adept.

Instinctively his body surged forward. A harsh sound of defeat rumbled in his chest as the incredible pleasure of her mouth wiped out all rational thought and reason. Dropping the sack which held her journal, he buried his fingers in her hair. *Later*, he decided, so turned on by Jade's boldness there was nothing he could do but surrender.

Somehow he managed to toe off his shoes. Jade discarded the rest of his clothing, her lips leaving no bared part of him uncharted. When he was finally naked, she stood, giving him one of the sexiest openmouthed kisses he'd ever had the pleasure of receiving. Without breaking the kiss, she pushed him back toward the bed until his legs hit the edge. The pressure of her hands on his chest was unrelenting, and he fell onto the mattress. She was right there with him, crawling on top of him, her moist heat dampening his skin as she sat astride his belly.

His breathing became labored. Wanting her as naked as he, he grasped the hem of her negligee and skimmed it up her thighs with trembling hands.

She shook her head and uttered, "No," then caught his wrists and pinned them at the sides of his head. Their position brought her breasts just inches from his face, and he took advantage of the offering. He nuzzled the softness, cursed the sheer material, but didn't let it hinder his exploration. His tongue flicked over a nipple, suckled her deep into his mouth.

She gasped and sat up, releasing his hands. Her expression softened with unabashed need and desire as she grabbed handfuls of the translucent material of her gown and slowly drew it up her thighs.

"Watch," she whispered, teasing him with the same command he'd used the first time they'd made love and he'd made her watch him strip off her panties.

It would have taken a major catastrophe for him to pry his eyes from her. She peeled the negligee over her head and tossed it aside. His gaze took in her supple, lean curves, her butterfly tattoo that seemed to flutter with each quivering breath, and the length of her firm legs straddling him. She was exquisite, her wildness and confidence lending her a sexiness that made his body tingle in excitement and anticipation.

Leaning over him and grazing his chest with the tips of her breasts, she kissed his jaw, his neck, sliding her bottom lower, until his thickened erection encountered wet silk and slick heat. Lower still and he slid into the tight sheath of her body, a flawless fit. Flexing her thighs against his hips, she sat up and arched into him, burying the length of him to the hilt.

Their mutual groans of gratification filled the dim room. Masculine instinct urged him to touch her, but he refrained from that particular temptation. This was her seduction. And being at Jade's mercy, he realized, was awesomely fulfilling. Through heavy-lidded eyes, he watched as she rode him, rocking against him. Slowly. Rhythmically. Sinuously.

Then she looked down and met his gaze. A sultry smile curved her mouth. Her golden green eyes glowed with heat, passion...and love. It was a wondrous, overwhelming feeling being on the receiving end of such emotion...and it was that reverence, that total trust, that sent him over the edge. With a mighty groan he gave himself over to the breathless pleasure, let her take him places he'd never been before. Places he'd merely dreamed existed.

At length, the tempest ended and she lay wrapped in his embrace all sleepy warm and replete. When she whispered in his ear that she loved him, he prayed she'd still feel the same once he came clean with her.

JADE STEPPED from the bathroom after taking a hot morning shower, expecting to find Kyle in bed sleeping, where she'd left him half an hour ago. He was gone, but the sounds from the kitchen and the smell of fresh coffee assured her he hadn't snuck out.

Not that she expected him to, she thought as she chose a casual summer dress from her closet and slipped it over her head. Several times last night he'd told her they needed to talk, but she hadn't been in a chatting kind of mood. Much to her delight, Kyle had been easily distracted and extremely accommodating of the erotic requests and wicked fantasies she'd whispered in his ear. Making love with Kyle would never be boring, not when they complemented one another so perfectly. Not when he seemed to know exactly what she wanted, what she needed, even before she did.

This morning, however, feeling refreshed and rejuvenated and hopelessly in love, she was actually anticipating their discussion. Their relationship had evolved beyond a casual affair into something more intimate and wondrous. And for the first time in years she'd begun to think of the possibility of marriage and a family of her own, and wondered how Kyle felt about those things.

Smiling at the possibilities, she picked up his scattered clothes from the floor, folded them, and put them on her dresser. She bent to retrieve his belt, caught sight of the knapsack he'd brought with him last night, and picked that up, too. Expecting something light, like a change of clothes, the bulkiness she encountered caught her by surprise. Curiosity roused, she unsnapped the front closure, opened the flap, and reached inside the canvas tote.

She frowned as her fingers slid over a smooth surface, then closed around the binding of a book. Unable to understand why Kyle would bring over a book, hidden in a knapsack no less, she pulled it out.

And froze. The knapsack slipped from her hand and dropped to the floor as she stared at the burgundy bound journal that looked exactly like the one she'd been missing. The back of her neck tingled in apprehension, disbelief clashing with the awful, growing suspicion.

Denial was not powerful enough to stop her from opening the front cover. Her name, written inside, confirmed the horrible, devastating truth.

The journal was hers. And Kyle had had it in his possession.

A low, painful moan escaped her. She began to tremble, the unbearable quaking starting deep inside her soul and working its way outward, making her hand shake uncontrollably. Reeling from the knowledge, she thought about the various times Kyle had seduced her, about the similarities between those times together and her fantasies, about how he'd seemed to know her so well. Her intimate thoughts. Her most personal, private secrets.

She felt exposed. Naked. And betrayed.

She drew in a ragged breath that caught sharply in her throat. Their relationship, his love, was all a lie. She'd been nothing more than a challenge to Kyle, one he'd conquered with such incredible ease. Through her fantasies he'd controlled her responses and influenced her emotions. And she'd fallen for his ploy. For him. For the second time in her life she'd played the fool to a man. She'd trusted his word and her judgment, only to discover that when it came to men, her perception of who they were missed the mark by a mile. Would she never learn?

Humiliation burned through her veins, hot and molten. She hated herself for not seeing the obvious, for not figuring out the truth by listening to that niggling voice inside her head. But she hated Kyle more for taking advantage of her and her journal of fantasies. She held fast to that glimmer of anger until the demoralizing feeling within her faded, crystalizing into a blazing fury.

Her body snapped taut, ready to do battle. This time, *she* was going to be in control of how this farce of a relationship ended.

"Coffee's ready, tiger," Kyle said from behind her as he came into her bedroom. "You interested in a cup?"

Jade didn't think, just reacted in a purely emotional manner. Whirling around, she closed the short distance separating them and slapped him across the face, hard enough to make his head snap to the side and her palm sting. "You son of a bitch," she said vehemently. "How could you do something so vile and despicable?" She didn't give him a chance to answer; then again he looked too stunned by her greeting to speak. She took advantage of his silence to vent her rage. "But then maybe that's the problem. You don't have any morals, do you? You were just out for a good time and I became an easy target."

Absently he touched his flaming cheek with light fingertips. "What are you talking about?" he asked, though his low voice was fringed with enough caution that Jade suspected he already knew what she was referring to.

"This." She lifted the incriminating evidence, resisting the urge to bash the book over his goddamned gorgeous head. "Look familiar? It's a personal, *private* journal of fantasies, Kyle. *My* fantasies. And look," she said in mock surprise as she opened the cover and shoved it so close to his face he went cross-eyed. "It even has my name in it, so someone *honest* could return it before it got into the wrong hands."

He pushed the book away and met her gaze, a muscle in his jaw tightening. There was something in his eyes—

regret? Surely not, she thought bitterly. Someone who calculated such a depraved scheme couldn't be capable of such an emotion.

"Jade—"

"Where did you get it?" she asked abruptly, not wanting to hear lies and flimsy excuses. "I want the truth, if you're able to give me at least that."

Her insult wasn't lost on him. "It was in the box of books I bought at the yard sale."

Somehow she'd known, even though her mind had tossed out that likelihood because she hadn't wanted to accept the possibility. In a tight, aching voice she asked, "Did you know the journal was in the box before you bought the books?"

He hesitated, his whole body taut and defensive, though the denial she expected never formulated. "Yes."

She turned away, squeezing her eyes shut, trying to block the pain ripping her insides to shreds. So, his pursuit had been deliberate, spurred by her most intimate fantasies. And like someone desperate for attention, starved for affection, she'd succumbed to his scheme.

She shuddered to realize how incredibly naive she'd been. Again.

"Jade, I'd like a chance to explain."

She spun back around, shooting him an incredulous look. "What's there to explain?" she asked, tossing the journal onto the rumpled bed. "Besides the fact that you used my fantasies to exploit me, physically and emotionally?"

If she hadn't been staring so intently at his face while issuing her challenge, she would have missed the way he'd winced at her cutting words. "When I first discovered your journal, I saw it as an opportunity to get to know you better."

"It was an invasion of privacy!" she said, her voice shrill to her own ears. "You took those fantasies and twisted them into your own sick, perverted versions."

He jammed his hands on his hips, his fingers biting into the waistband of his boxer shorts. And then he had the gall to glare at her. "It was *never* like that!"

"Wasn't it?" she cried in outrage. The injustice was hers, dammit, and she wasn't about to relinquish it to him. "What about the night at the pool? Or the incident in your office with the peaches? And then there was the time you whispered in my ear, 'put your hands on the table and keep them there,' and then proceeded to imitate a fantasy I'd written. Oh, and let's not forget your romantic adventure, and you bathing me in a very familiar way." Her face burned with the humiliating memories, the way she'd openly responded to him. Accepted him. Trusted him. And gradually fallen in love with him.

It was all a ruse.

She jerked her chin up mutinously. "Did you or did you not buy my journal with the intention of using the fantasies to seduce me?"

His chest rose and fell on a harsh breath. His gaze was bright with self-condemnation, but the silent acknowledgment wasn't enough for her. She was hurting, the sting of betrayal making her ruthless.

"Dammit, answer me!" she said furiously. "Did you?"

"Yes," he hissed, the admission forced from him reluctantly. He clawed his fingers through his hair, the gesture filled with frustration. "I did, at first. It all seemed innocent enough—"

She gaped at him. "You call manipulating someone's emotions innocent? Tell me, did you read my fantasies and feel sorry for me? Am I some kind of charity case you decided to take pity on? Poor Jade, she's so uptight she's got to write fantasies instead of finding herself a real man," she mocked.

Blue eyes blazing with indignation, he caught her by the shoulders and gave her a firm shake. "For Christ's sake, Jade, I *never* felt sorry for you! I was attracted to you, and although I knew you were attracted to me, too, you never let your guard down long enough to give me a chance. Then I found your journal, and I began to understand why you were so cautious. Your fantasies were safe, a way for you to escape without the threat of being hurt. Those fantasies allowed me to get close enough to discover who the *real* Jade was."

Embarrassed that he'd seen so much in her journal entries, she shrugged off his touch. "And in the meantime, you had great fun playing fantasy lover, didn't you?" At her emotional expense. "Tell me, did you enjoy messing with my head, confusing reality and fantasy? Just last night you came into my bedroom through my balcony, just like a fantasy I'd written! And you brought my journal with you. Were you hoping we could snuggle under the covers and read them together?" she asked sarcastically.

He took her barbed words with grace and admirable calm. "I came over last night with every intention of giving back the journal."

Her face warmed as she recalled how she'd distracted him, and what a fool she'd made of herself by telling him she loved him. "And your great noble gesture was supposed to make everything you've done okay?" Certainly he didn't think she was *that* guileless. Or forgiving.

"No, it wasn't," he said succinctly. Finding his folded clothes on her dresser, he grabbed his slacks and yanked them on, his gaze never leaving her face. "But did it ever occur to you that if I hadn't brought over that journal, you never would have known I had it?" He let that realization sink in while zipping up his pants and fastening the button. "I didn't *have* to give it back, Jade. I could have held on to it, or thrown it away, and you never would have known. It was *my* choice to give it back."

She didn't want to give him the chance to redeem himself, but she found she couldn't keep from asking the all-important question: "So why did you?"

He approached her, his expression tenacious, and though every instinct urged her to step away, she found she couldn't. He framed her face in his hands, his grasp gentle as he tilted her chin up, leaving her no choice but to look deeply into his eyes. She saw a wealth of regret, too much warmth and caring, and a need for her understanding she resolutely ignored.

"Why did I decide to give back the journal?" he said, repeating her question. "Because when I fell in love with you, I realized what I did was wrong, and I didn't want the deception between us."

She didn't want to believe him, didn't want to fall for more lies. No, she wanted to hurt him the same way she was hurting. "Guilt is a pretty powerful emotion, isn't it?" From what she knew, it had been driving him for seventeen years.

He looked taken aback by her low blow, but recovered in the next instant. "Yeah, it is," he said gruffly. "I've done a lot of things in my life I'm not proud of, and more things I regret. That's why I see the importance of being totally honest with you."

She smirked. "By doing the *responsible* thing?"

"Yes." His mouth tightened into a grim line. "Goddammit, Jade, I don't want to lose you!"

"And I'd be stupid to believe you!" Needing space, she shoved away from him, but before she could put any distance between them he grabbed her arm and whirled her back around.

"Believe this," he said fiercely. "I never meant to hurt you. I love you, Jade."

To her horror, she felt tears burn the back of her throat. She wrenched her arm from his grasp and embraced her furious emotions. "You have a hell of a way of showing it. Or was that just a game to you, too? Fulfill my fantasies, tell me you love me and then see if I'll be grateful enough, stupid enough, to declare undying devotion in return?"

Anger flashed in his eyes, turning them to a steely shade of blue. "I'll admit I never expected to fall in love with you, but I've never lied about my feelings for you. Not once."

"I did," she said hurtfully, bitterly. "I don't love you. I *hate* you." Feeling raw and torn inside, she wrapped her arms around her middle, wanting to let the awful tension within her unravel, but not in front of Kyle. There'd be plenty of time for that later, when she was alone. "I trusted you, and you betrayed me in the worst way possible."

She watched him struggle with the truth of that statement, but there was no way he could refute the fact that he *had* taken advantage of her. "Jade," he implored, stepping toward her once again.

She backed away, holding up her hand as if the gesture alone would keep him at bay. "I don't want to hear any more," she choked out, damning the tears that now filled her eyes. "Just leave me alone. You had your fun, and I'll admit the sex was fantastic, but I guess I'm not cut out for a no-strings-attached affair."

He didn't argue, though it appeared it took effort to restrain himself. "I'll go, for now," he relented, swiping up the rest of his clothes.

Without another word, he left, closing the front door after him. She leaned against the wall for support, but her shaking legs gave out anyway. Sliding to the floor, she buried her face in her hands and gave into the sobs she'd been holding back. The raw pain erupted within her, clawing at her heart until she feared nothing was left.

Oh, God. She'd succeeded. She'd maintained control of the situation. She'd ended her relationship with Kyle with dignity. So why did she feel as though she'd lost everything that mattered to her?

11

SHE WAS LATE.

Kyle checked his watch for the fourth time in the past fifteen minutes, then glanced out one of the windows in the lounge, waiting for a sporty red Miata to pull into the parking lot. According to the conversation he'd had with Jade's secretary a few days ago, he had a 10:00 a.m. appointment to have pictures taken of the refurbished bar and restaurant for Casual Elegance's portfolio. When he'd nonchalantly asked if Jade would be there for the shoot, he'd been told that she did usually accompany the photographer.

After a week apart, and with Jade so expertly avoiding him, he saw this opportunity as his one chance to talk to her. He'd been a wreck since he'd walked out of her condo. Leaving to give her space had been his biggest mistake—the closest he'd gotten to her since that morning was to hear her voice on her answering machine, on which he'd left a reel of messages she hadn't returned.

His hopes of any sort of reconciliation dwindled when a champagne-colored BMW turned into the lot. A minute later, Mariah slid from the car, followed by a dark-haired man who emerged from the passenger side. He retrieved a large canvas bag and other photography paraphernalia from the trunk, then the two of them headed toward the entrance.

He waited at the door, feeling more than a little disgruntled that Jade had sent her sister to escort the photographer. As Mariah neared, he tried to gauge her mood, not sure what Jade had told her of their breakup.

The photographer entered the establishment first, his gaze quickly assessing the place before settling on Kyle. "'Morning," he said pleasantly.

Kyle gave him a brief nod of greeting, and the other man strolled past him and into the lounge area of the bar. Setting his bag on a table, he began unzipping compartments, pulling out a camera, lenses, film and other items.

Mariah stopped in front of him, boldly meeting his gaze. There was no animosity in her blue eyes, just a mild scrutiny he wasn't sure he liked or appreciated. His frown deepened.

"Hello, Mariah," he said, breaking the silence that was beginning to grate on his nerves as much as her unsettling inspection. Instinctively he braced himself for the scathing upbraiding sure to come in her sister's defense.

"You look disappointed to see me." A satisfied smile played around her lips. "I suppose that's a good sign."

He blinked at her unexpectedly blithe comment. "It's nothing personal," he said, forcing his tense shoulders to relax. "I was hoping to see Jade, but I should have known better than to think she'd come today when she's managed to avoid me for an entire week."

"No offense taken," she assured him. "At least now I know you really do care about Jade."

His jaw tightened with annoyance. "Of course I care about her." He loved the stubborn, sassy woman so much he ached at the thought of losing her. Yet he didn't know how to gain her forgiveness, especially when she refused to take his calls or see him.

Mariah glanced at the photographer, who looked ready to begin his assignment. "John, go ahead and start with the restaurant. You know what Jade expects in a portfolio, so I'll trust your judgment."

"Will do, boss," he said, and disappeared through the archway adjoining the bar and dining area.

Clasping her hands behind her back, Mariah strolled casually around the lounge, her gaze taking in the improvements. "Truth be told, after what Jade told me you did, I did have my doubts about you and your intentions."

"She told you what happened?" he asked, feeling slightly uncomfortable that Jade would share something so personal, such as how he'd used her journal of fantasies to seduce her.

Mariah glanced over her shoulder at him. "Don't be so surprised, Kyle. We're like best friends, and share just about everything. But seeing that you look as miserable as she does, I have to believe there's something more between the two of you than just a journal of fantasies."

He took little comfort in the fact that Jade was feeling as bleak as he was. "I never meant to hurt her, Mariah. I'll admit what I did was wrong—"

"Not to mention immoral," she added.

"Well, yes," he reluctantly agreed.

"And unconscionable."

Unable to refute that, he gave a brisk nod. "Yes."

"And downright underhanded."

He scowled and jammed his hands on his hips. The woman was pushing it, but he couldn't argue the truth. "Yes."

"And dishonest."

Hell, at this rate, he might as well incriminate himself one hundred percent. "Yes."

"And pretty darn close to being unforgivable."

He hesitated on that one. He didn't want to believe that

Jade would never forgive him. But Mariah was waiting, and wouldn't be satisfied until she had his remorse on a silver platter. "Yes! Yes, it was unforgivable."

"Just so long as we agree," she added sweetly.

"We agree," he promised irritably, anything to appease her. He continued before she interrupted him again. "But what happened as a result of finding that journal was something I wasn't prepared for, nor is it something I'm willing to give up on."

She raised an inquisitive brow. "And what happened?"

Kyle wasn't one to spill his guts about personal issues, but the need to talk to someone who understood the situation was overwhelming. He took advantage of Mariah's listening ear.

"I fell in love with the woman beneath the flashy clothes, colored contact lenses and sassiness. I discovered a woman who is so sweet and giving she makes me feel invincible and worthy. No one has ever touched me so deeply. I've never let anyone close enough to try." He scrubbed a hand through his hair and paced the newly varnished floor. "The truth is, the contents of that journal changed me."

She tilted her head, looking mildly surprised by his confession. "How so?"

"Those entries gave me so much insight into who Jade is, made me understand why she wouldn't let me, or any man get close to her. And while I was stripping away those layers of reserve, I came to care for Jade in ways I never expected."

Mariah digested that, then added very quietly, "She was hurt pretty badly in the past."

"I know all that. She told me everything. About how Adam destroyed her self-confidence..." His voice trailed off as an awful realization hit him smack between the eyes. He'd never made the correlation between Adam's treachery and his own deception until now. Both of them had manipulated Jade in different ways, wringing her out emotionally and destroying her trust. Christ, was it no wonder she loathed him?

He swallowed that truth, but it was a bitter pill to choke down. "Jade probably thinks I'm a bigger rat than Adam."

"Pretty darn close," Mariah agreed with a faint smile.

He had to laugh, just to release some of the pressure banding his chest. "Thanks. That makes me feel a helluva lot better." Feeling drained and defeated, he sank into a nearby chair and stared up at the ceiling fans whirling quietly in the lounge. His emotions were all jumbled, and try as he might, he couldn't ignore the huge ache in the vicinity of his heart.... A sensation he'd never experienced until he'd fallen in love.

Sighing heavily, he met Mariah's gaze again. "These past few months with Jade made me realize what was missing from my life. Laughter. Love. Caring. A family. I want things I've never wanted before...and I want them with Jade."

Mariah crossed her arms loosely over her chest, her expression delighted and pleased...and concerned. "Did you tell her this?"

"She won't give me the chance." He sat up straight and braced his elbows on his knees. "Hell, she won't answer her phone and she doesn't return the messages I leave for her, at home and at work. She won't even answer her door when I know damn well she's home!" He'd gotten a piece of her mail in his box the other day and had shoved it beneath her door, knowing there was little chance she'd allow him to deliver it in person. "I'm running out of options, Mariah, and the more time that passes, the more she's going to grow to hate me."

"She's hurt, yes," Mariah said softly, and with the strength of wisdom that came from knowing her sibling so well. "But I know Jade also loves you. The only way she'll hate you is if you don't settle things between the two of you."

He stared at Mariah, wondering how in the world he was going to accomplish that mission when Jade refused any contact with him.

"Mariah," the photographer called, poking his head through the archway. "I need your advice on a couple of shots."

"I'll be right there, John," she said, though she didn't immediately head that way. Her gaze remained on Kyle. "She's convinced you used her, that the journal of fantasies she'd written was all just a game to you. Is that what you want her to think?" she asked, then left him to ponder that question.

Kyle's answer was immediate and crystal clear. *Hell, no!*

And then he groaned, realizing where he'd gone so horribly wrong. He'd told her he loved her, but he never said anything about wanting her in his life permanently. Never made her any of the promises she deserved.

No wonder she thought he'd used her.

Yet he had no idea how to make amends. He cursed the journal of fantasies, a part of him wishing he'd never laid hands on the damn book. But without it, he never would have known how warm and sweet Jade could be. Never would have known how good a woman's love could feel.

It was a catch-22 situation. That journal had been an essential part of their relationship. It had taken him to the heights of passion—and the depths of despair.

The journal.

An idea came to him then, and he smiled, experiencing the first glimmer of hope in a week's time. It was outrageous what he was thinking. A long shot, really. But it was his only hope of repairing the damage he'd done.

He was going to rekindle their relationship the same way it had begun two months ago.

THE BULKY PACKAGE JAMMED into Jade's mailbox fell to the floor the moment she opened the small metal door. Cursing the new mail-carrier-in-training on her route for over-stuffing her box, she grabbed the rest of her mail before it fluttered to the ground as well. Since it was Saturday evening, she'd have to wait until Monday morning to file a complaint.

Blowing out an aggravated stream of breath, and ignoring the package at her feet for the moment, she quickly skimmed through the mail in her hands. She paused when she came across a utility bill addressed to Kyle, her stomach clenching with dread. She'd been waiting for this to happen and knew the best way to handle the situation was to slip the envelope under his door when he wasn't home, just like he'd done with hers. And at the same time she could return the key to his condo that he'd given her only days before their fight.

She remembered thinking how thrilled she'd been by the overture, how hopeful she'd been about them, their relationship and their future. Now she wasn't likely to need the key ever again.

She couldn't avoid Kyle forever, she knew, not when they lived in the same complex. But she wasn't prepared to face him again, either. The first time was bound to be extremely strained, and emotionally charged, and until she figured out how to handle the awkward situation, she chose to take extra precautions to avoid him.

She couldn't imagine shunning Kyle, because they'd more than likely be neighbors for years to come. But reverting to the flirtatious, casual relationship they'd established before their affair wasn't a possibility. She wasn't sure where that left them...as acquaintances? That seemed so impersonal after everything they'd shared, yet too familiar when she forced herself to remember the way he'd manipulated her. She'd finally decided it was safest just to think of him as a Casual Elegance client.

The anger and humiliation had faded over the past two weeks, leaving behind a hole brimming with aching misery. She wanted to hate Kyle, but her heart wouldn't let her off the hook so easily. Despite what he'd done, she missed him. Missed the warmth and closeness they'd shared. And at night, she ached for his touch, and the way he'd make her come alive with a whispered word, a fleeting caress.

But she couldn't forget his deception. The silent lies. Couldn't forget that he'd taken her private fantasies and intimate secrets and deliberately used them to seduce her.

The way he'd exploited her was unforgivable.

So why was she having such a difficult time accepting that truth?

Not wanting to analyze the conflicting emotions that had been troubling her since she'd ordered Kyle out of her life, she relocked her mailbox and picked up the padded manila envelope on the floor. Heading back toward her condo, she glanced at the front of the package and frowned. Her name and address were typed on a plain white label, but there wasn't a return address, which she found extremely odd. She hadn't ordered anything recently through the mail, and even when she did she had those items delivered to the office because of her small mailbox.

Once inside the privacy of her home, she dropped her keys and regular mail on her dinette table and tore open the flap on the mystery envelope. Curious, yet cautious, she dumped the contents instead of reaching blindly inside the package. An emerald green leather-bound journal landed with a distinct *thump* on the table.

Jade's heart leapt into her throat, then beat at a frantic pace that made her blood roar in her ears. Embossed on the cover in gold lettering were the names Kyle And Jade, along with the year. There was no letter attached, nothing to explain why she'd been sent this journal, though she didn't need a note to know who it was from.

Kyle.

The tug-of-war of emotions she'd been trying so hard to control began to overtake her, wearing down her resistance against the man who had betrayed her. Try as she might to cling to any remnant of anger, her heart was unable to ignore the possibilities tied to such a gift. Despite being hurt, she wanted to believe in Kyle and what they shared. She wanted to *hope.*

Picking up the journal, she opened the front cover. Written inside in Kyle's bold handwriting was a short dedication:

To Jade,
To fill with a lifetime of fantasies and memories.
> Love, Kyle

Feeling light-headed, she sank into the nearest chair and reread those words, not sure she understood their meaning, or what Kyle was implying. Idly she fanned through the sheets of lined paper, all of them blank until she came to the first page. She read the message Kyle had written there.

You're everything I've ever dreamed of in a woman, but never knew I needed until you came into my life. I wasn't looking for love, but unexpectedly found it with you.

I see you as my best friend, someone who knows my deepest secrets, fears and failures and accepts me for who I am. I see you beside me as my wife, sharing my life and all the trials and triumphs that go with it. I see you as my lover, warm, passionate and sexy...a tiger through and through. I see you as the mother of our children, patient, loving and kind.

I see us as a family. Growing old together. Sharing laughter and making memories. A commitment bonded with the strength of love and respect.

I need you in my life, and in my future.

This is my fantasy. I want it to be reality with you.

Jade closed the journal and hugged it to her chest, the last line of his entry echoing in her mind and her heart. Emotions she'd tried so hard to suppress filled her empty soul until it ached and tightened her throat with tears.

His entry was so simple, yet so powerful. There was no sappy apology, and he hadn't begged, cajoled or pleaded with her. No, that wasn't Kyle's style. The fantasy was written in the same bold, straightforward way he approached life. The same daring way he'd pursued her—except this time he was risking his own heart, and the possibility of a final rejection.

He was giving her a choice. No manipulation tactics, no demands, no coercion. He'd bared his soul, laying his feelings at her feet. It was up to her whether she accepted the gift he offered, or clung to the hurt and betrayal, and rebuffed his attempt to gain her forgiveness, and her love.

And she did love him. Enough to forgive him. Enough to believe he'd never, ever deliberately hurt her.

Enough to admit he was nothing like Adam.

She drew a shaky breath and stared down at the journal. The two men, and each circumstance, were incomparable. Adam had dominated and controlled her, physically and emotionally. Kyle had discovered through her fantasies, the vulnerable woman beneath the facade she presented to the rest of the world. He'd catered to that woman's needs, gently coaxing, patiently waiting for her to gain the confidence she needed to break past her fears and trust a man again.

Without the intimate knowledge her journal provided, she wouldn't have let him close.

And while Adam had scorned her and walked away from their relationship without a backward glance, Kyle was still around, fighting for her. For *them*, if his entry in the emerald green journal was any indication.

Touching her fingers to the gold lettering on the cover, she absently traced their names. It was easier to cling to her resentment than to confront the truth. It was so much easier to blame Kyle than to face her fears. And it was too easy to hide behind fantasies than jeopardize her heart.

But she already had. Her heart was already his. Now she risked losing Kyle.

Unwilling to face a future without him, she stood and headed toward her bedroom, knowing there was one final thing she needed to do before she accepted Kyle's gift. Withdrawing her burgundy and sapphire blue journals from her nightstand, she put them away in a floral packing box on the top shelf in her closet.

It was time she stopped hiding behind her fantasies and accepted reality. And her love for Kyle.

HE WAS GOING CRAZY. There was no other explanation for the faint scent of peaches that greeted him when he opened the door to his condo. For a moment he closed his eyes and stood there, just beyond the threshold, certain the scent that reminded him so much of Jade was an illusion and would dissipate once he entered his home. Unwilling to let go of his own personal fantasy just yet, he breathed in the heady fragrance. The essence wrapped around him, soothing and arousing at the same time.

He hadn't heard from Jade since sending the journal days ago, and though male instinct urged him to confront her and find out where he stood, he wasn't about to push her into something she didn't want or wasn't ready for. The decision to accept him, to forgive him, had to be hers. And he had to trust in her enough to believe she would make the right choice. The only choice.

Keeping that confident thought foremost in his mind, he stepped into his house, closed the door, and came to an abrupt stop again. His heart thudded heavily in his chest as he took in the scene before him.

His small dining table had been draped with cream linen and was set for two with fine china and delicate crystal. A platter of shrimp, meats, cheeses, fresh fruits and croissants graced the table, along with a silver bucket of ice chilling a bottle of champagne. Soft background music played, and the drapes had been drawn, closing out the rest of the world. Two taper candles in the center of the table cast the room in intimate shadows, and he noticed that the emerald green journal was placed between the settings, opened to a blank page with a pen resting in the spine's crease.

His gaze gradually moved to another vision, this one of the woman who stood nearby. She wore a white, old-fashioned lace dress that fell to her calves in a feminine swirl of material, and gave way to soft, white leather lace-up boots.

She looked like a dream. So much so that he feared that everything before him was an apparition. But then a tremulous sigh escaped her and she shifted anxiously on her feet, breaking the ethereal spell.

"Hi," she said, her wobbly, uncertain voice shaking him out of his trance.

He blinked, and afraid to assume anything, asked, "What's all this for?"

A slight, nervous kind of smile touched the corner of her mouth. "I'm starting where your fantasy left off."

Oh, man. Elation filled him to near bursting. It would be so simple to close the distance between them, pull her into his arms and kiss her senseless. But there were still unresolved issues between them and he didn't want the exquisite feel and sweet taste of her to distract him from what still needed to be said.

He held her gaze, the gold flecks in her eyes glimmering from the candlelight. "Are you certain that's what you want?"

"More certain than I've been of anything in a long time."

"So, you forgive me?" he asked guardedly, part of him still afraid to believe.

"Yes." Her answer was strong and clear. So was the hopeful racing of his heart.

He started toward her, slow and easy. "And you know I never meant to hurt you?"

Her chest rose and fell with a deep breath. "Yes."

"And you know there's nothing I can say or do that will change what I did?"

"Yes," she whispered.

He stopped in front of her, and asked the most important question of all. "Do you believe I love you?"

"Yes." Her verbal response matched the breathtaking smile on her face. "Do you believe I love you?"

"Yeah, I do," he said huskily, humbled by that simple, precious gift. Love wasn't something he'd had much experience with in his life, but it was proving to be a powerful, all-encompassing emotion. An emotion he wanted to share with the woman who made him so whole and complete. The one woman who'd made a difference in his life.

Words were suddenly inadequate to express how he was feeling. He needed to *show* her...and did, by cradling the back of her head in his palm and lifting her mouth to his. His lips skimmed hers, soft and supple. Their tongues met, and he tasted warm, honeyed peaches and the flavor of forever.

He dragged his mouth from hers, and looked into her eyes. "Ah, Jade, I've never felt like this before. Never dreamed I could want or need someone so much."

"Kyle—"

He pressed his fingers to her soft, damp lips, not wanting her to interrupt him. "All my life I've avoided commitment and relationships because it was so much easier being alone. I had no one's expectations to live up to, didn't have to worry about trying to please someone—or worse, failing like I have in the past. I was so convinced I didn't need anyone. But I do need you, Jade. I need the way you believe in me and accept me for who I am."

She pulled his hand away, understanding shimmering in her eyes. "I think we need each other."

He liked the way that sounded. A whole lot. "And I want things with you that I've never had. A future. A family."

A troubled frown marred her brow, and he smoothed his thumb over the wrinkle, but it didn't go away. "What?" he asked, concerned. "You don't want that?"

She worried her bottom lip between her teeth. "You really want children, even though you have a daughter that's nearly an adult?"

He chuckled, relieved. "I'd take a half a dozen if that's what you wanted. I want babies, Jade. I want to watch them grow up and I want to be there for them like I've never been there for Christy. I'm the first to admit I wasn't ready for a family at eighteen, but I think I'm ready now, and I want that, and I want it with you. Only you."

"Yes." She wrapped her arms around his neck and pulled him down for another kiss, this one long and deep and packed with so much emotion it nearly brought him to his knees.

When they finally came up for air, she pressed her palm against his cheek, touching him reverently. "I was so afraid of trusting you," she admitted. "Afraid of being controlled again and losing my identity. But you complemented me in a way that no one ever has before, made me feel alive and more confident about myself."

"And what about your fantasies?" he asked.

"I put them away, where they belong." She smiled, the self-assurance she spoke of lighting her eyes. "I was hiding behind those fantasies, because I feared being manipulated again. But you've given me a greater freedom and confidence to express myself, with no pretenses."

Grasping the hand on his cheek, he pressed a warm kiss in the center of her palm. "That's the way it should be."

She sighed as he gently nipped at the sensitive pad of flesh just below her thumb, then soothed the playful lovebite with his tongue. "It's the way it is with you.

You're the only fantasy man and lover I'll ever want, and our journal is the only one we'll ever need."

He eyed the emerald green journal on the table. "It's going to be a big job trying to fill it with fantasies."

She tilted her head back and laughed huskily, sexily, as her hand smoothed over the zipper of his jeans and lovingly cupped the fullness there. "Oh, I do believe you're up to the challenge."

He groaned as his manhood swelled in her grasp. Maneuvering her closer to the table, he reached behind her and impatiently pushed the place settings, food and candles to the opposite end of the table, clearing a spot. "It'll probably be filled within a week."

She gasped, her eyes widening in surprise when he scooted her bottom onto the edge of the table. "Then we'll buy another one."

Grinning wickedly, he moved between her knees and skimmed his hands up her calves, then beneath the hem of her dress, slowly pushing the material up her silky, bare thighs. "You know," he began in a low, provocative murmur, "I've had this fantasy of making love to you on my dining table, all spread out for me to feast on...." He wiggled his brows lasciviously. "How does that fantasy sound for our first entry?"

"Fulfill it, and I'll let you know," she dared impudently.

He chuckled, knowing he'd never tire of this woman's sass, her fire, her passion. "It would be my pleasure." Grasping the sides of her very flimsy panties, he pulled them over her hips and down her legs, tossing them somewhere over his shoulder. But before he could touch her intimately, she caught his wrist and halted him inches away from his goal.

"Oh, I almost forgot, Mr. Stephens," she said, her voice a beguiling mixture of teasing charm and breathless need.

He lifted a brow, playing along with her game. "What's that, Ms. Stevens?"

She twisted enough to reach for something within the folds of the tablecloth behind her. Facing him again, she tapped an envelope against his chest and blew out an indignant stream of breath. "I got another piece of *your* mail in *my* mailbox."

With his free hand he plucked the bill away and took a brief moment to contemplate the situation. "You know, there's really only one thing to do about this mix-up with our last names and addresses."

Her lashes fell half-mast as his captured fingers drew lazy patterns on the inside of her thigh. "And what's that?"

"Marry me, and make my fantasy come true."

An ecstatic smile curved her mouth, and her eyes glowed with delight. "Now there's a fantasy I'd be more than happy to fulfill."

HARLEQUIN®

Temptation

It's a dating wasteland out there! So what's a girl to do when there's not a marriage-minded man in sight? Go hunting, of course.

Manhunting

Enjoy the hilarious antics of five intrepid heroines, determined to lead Mr. Right to the altar— whether he wants to go or not!

#669 *Manhunting in Memphis—*
Heather MacAllister (February 1998)

#673 *Manhunting in Manhattan—*
Carolyn Andrews (March 1998)

#677 *Manhunting in Montana—*
Vicki Lewis Thompson (April 1998)

#681 *Manhunting in Miami—*
Alyssa Dean (May 1998)

#685 *Manhunting in Mississippi—*
Stephanie Bond (June 1998)

She's got a plan—to find herself a man!

Available wherever Harlequin books are sold.

Take 2 bestselling love stories FREE

Plus get a FREE surprise gift!

Special Limited-Time Offer

Mail to Harlequin Reader Service®

3010 Walden Avenue
P.O. Box 1867
Buffalo, N.Y. 14240-1867

YES! Please send me 2 free Harlequin Temptation® novels and my free surprise gift. Then send me 4 brand-new novels every month, which I will receive before they appear in bookstores. Bill me at the low price of $3.12 each plus 25¢ delivery and applicable sales tax, if any.* That's the complete price, and a saving of over 10% off the cover prices—quite a bargain! I understand that accepting the books and gift places me under no obligation ever to buy any books. I can always return a shipment and cancel at any time. Even if I never buy another book from Harlequin, the 2 free books and the surprise gift are mine to keep forever.

142 HEN CH7G

Name _____ (PLEASE PRINT)

Address _____ Apt. No. _____

City _____ State _____ Zip _____

This offer is limited to one order per household and not valid to present Harlequin Temptation® subscribers. *Terms and prices are subject to change without notice. Sales tax applicable in N.Y.

UTEMP-98

©1990 Harlequin Enterprises Limited

DEBBIE MACOMBER

invites you to the

HEART OF TEXAS

Join Debbie Macomber as she brings you the lives
and loves of the folks in the ranching community
of Promise, Texas.

If you loved Midnight Sons—don't miss
Heart of Texas! A brand-new six-book series
from Debbie Macomber.

Available in February 1998
at your favorite retail store.

Heart of Texas by Debbie Macomber

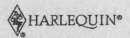

HARLEQUIN®

HPHRT1

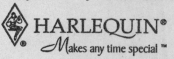

It's hot...
and it's out of control!

**This summer, Temptation turns up the heat.
Look for these bold, provocative,
ultra-sexy books!**

#686 *SEDUCING SULLIVAN*
Julie Elizabeth Leto
June 1998

Angela Harris had only one obsession—Jack Sullivan.
Ever since high school, he'd been on her mind...and
in her fantasies. But no more. At her ten-year
reunion, she was going to get him out of her system
for good. All she needed was one sizzling night with
Jack—and then she could get on with her life.
Unfortunately she hadn't counted on Jack having a
few obsessions of his own....

BLAZE! Red-hot reads from

HARLEQUIN®

Temptation®

COMING NEXT MONTH